RED, WHITE
★ ★ ★ ★ & ★ ★ ★ ★
ARMY BLUE

RED, WHITE
★ ★ ★ ★ ★ & ★ ★ ★ ★ ★
ARMY BLUE

PETER R. DECKER

This is a work of fiction. Names, characters, organizations, places, events, and incidents are either products of the author's imagination or are used fictitiously.

Published by Western Slope Press
Denver, Colorado
www.westernslopepress.com

Edited and designed by Girl Friday Productions
www.girlfridayproductions.com
Interior and cover design: Paul Barrett

ISBN-13: 9780692278062
ISBN-10: 0692278060

First Edition

Printed in the United States of America

To my children: Karen, Christopher, and Hilary

ONE

Corporal Hiram Marlow knew the dream well. It began as Marlow led his 4th Cavalry troopers into a rocky ravine toward the bottom of the Palo Duro Canyon, where they hoped to encounter the Comanche responsible for the summer massacre of white settlers moving by wagon train across the Texas Panhandle. He was acting as point man fifty yards in front of his squad and halfway down the steep ravine when his horse took an arrow in the neck and another in the ribs. The horse stumbled; Marlow hit the ground hard as his mount fell on him. Two Comanche sprang from their hideout.

The two young braves, their faces painted with crimson stripes, dragged him from under his injured horse. One jumped on his chest; the other sat on his legs. Marlow heard a sound like a chicken's skin being torn off its breast and felt the pain as his scalp separated from his skull. And then another deep shock of pain, this one bolting through his entire body, as the second Indian sliced off his testicles and then stuffed them down Marlow's throat.

Marlow's body stiffened as he gagged for air.

He heard the notes of a bugle outside his tent farting out reveille. With one hand he touched his head. His other hand went to his crotch.

As Corporal Marlow shook himself awake, he remembered he was no longer in Texas but in western Colorado's Uncompahgre River Valley at an Army cantonment, guarding one of three bands of Ute Indians on their twelve-million-acre reservation. The small Army post sat adjacent to the Los Piños Indian Agency, the administrative arm of Washington's Bureau of Indian Affairs responsible for the fifteen hundred Uncompahgre Ute under the agency's jurisdiction. Located in the middle of a twenty-mile-long grass valley, the cantonment caught all the winter winds spilling over the thousand-foot mesas to the east and west. The snow-capped mountains to the south, with peaks over fourteen thousand feet, attracted little attention from the soldiers except as a predictor of summer rains or winter storms. The Utes chose the valley because of its belly-high-to-a-pony grass and nearby water from the Uncompahgre River. The Army and Indian Bureau chose the site for the presence of the Ute.

Marlow, a short, stocky, muscular young man of twenty-six, had volunteered in 1875 for the cavalry from his home state of Iowa. His sandy hair, cut short, framed a handsome face, marred only by a crooked nose and a small forehead scar, the result of horse accidents in his early years. He possessed the broad, sloping shoulders and muscular chest and arms of someone who'd spent much of his youth on the working end of a two- or four-hitch gangplow. He was equally proficient with a seed planter, cutter bar, rake, or the newest baler. His skills included the repair of the machinery and the training of the farm's saddle and work-horses. He had learned valuable horse-training skills from a hired hand, Bobby, a Dakota Sioux. These skills he took to the enlistment center at Kansas City and later to the cavalry training center at Fort Riley, Kansas.

Marlow hoped the day's schedule would include his favorite horse drills. In the saber drill, he galloped his mount toward a straw figure dressed as an Indian. With his saber drawn and pointed at the target, he either speared the chest or slashed at the neck, all while the drill instructor yelled, "*Kill, kill, kill!*" In the pistol drill, Marlow, his horse at a fast gallop, could fire off two shots and hit the small wooden target from twenty-five yards. And with his carbine, again in a gallop, he'd coordinate his riding with the stride of his horse to fire off a .45-caliber bullet at a horse-shaped target thirty yards distant. Rigorous drills would keep him warm even in this weather.

Inside the mildewed two-man tent, Marlow broke the ice in the tin cup next to his cot and took a swallow to moisten his dry mouth. He checked to see if Mike Dolan, his tentmate, had heard the bugle. They pulled out of their bedrolls and rushed to dress in the cold air.

★　　★　　★

In preparation for the daily inspection on this September morning in Colorado, Marlow took his assigned position in C Company's formation. Company Sergeant O'Riley ordered the company to "*pre*-sent arms" before walking through the ranks scanning for filthy boots, a dirty blouse, or weapons with a spot of dirt or a speck of rust.

O'Riley had the reputation of a spit-and-polish sergeant. Marlow had once warned a new recruit that trying to pass an unpolished button by O'Riley's eye was like trying to sneak a sunrise by a sleeping rooster.

Simon O'Riley had joined a British cavalry unit at the age of sixteen, deserted, and immigrated to New York, where he gave his nationality as "famine Irish." During the Civil War, he served as a substitute for a wealthy New York City merchant in a Union cavalry unit for three years. From his English upper-class, polo-playing officers, whom he came to despise, he learned to appreciate well-muscled horses with good stamina and the skilled riders who could manage them. O'Riley recognized Marlow at once as one of the best in C Company.

Stopped before one young trooper, O'Riley noticed a button missing from his blue blouse. "Extra guard duty for you, trooper," O'Riley barked. To a recent recruit, he shouted, "Looks like a horse took a shit on your boots. In the next half hour, I want to see such a high polish on these boots that they reflect your ugly nose." From the next soldier, the sergeant grabbed his saber, slipped it out of its polished scabbard, and discovered a spot of rust on the blade. "If I ever see any rust on this saber again, I'll stick it up your arse and tickle your fugghan liver. Do I make myself understood, trooper?"

"Yes, Sarge."

He came up to Marlow. "Good-looking uniform," O'Riley said appraisingly. "Colorado treating you well, Marlow?"

"Sure is a lot cooler than Texas," Marlow said, "and I don't miss them Comanche."

"We sure as hell kicked their red-skinned arses down there," O'Riley answered.

"Real bad, Sarge."

"Are you prepared to do the same with the Ute here?"

"If they act up!"

O'Riley growled, "Trooper, it's not if, it's *when*. You can be certain they'll act up . . . so prepare yourself."

Marlow's frown and tight jaw displayed his unenthusiastic reaction to O'Riley's challenge. O'Riley moved to the head of the formation and ordered, "*Pa*-rade *rest*."

"Now listen up, you saddle pounders," O'Riley addressed the company. "We're part of a temporary infantry-cavalry regiment ordered to move these here Indians almost two-hundred-fifty miles into the Utah Territory, starting out at daylight tomorrow. You can bet your arse these Uncompahgre Ute are not happy about losing their homeland. And they're mighty pissed about us moving them to Utah. They may cause us some trouble along the way even though we've stripped them of their weapons.

"On the march, the two infantry companies and another cavalry company will be in the lead or on the flanks. We in C Company will guard the rear and put pressure on the Indians to keep the pace. Unfortunately, it also means we'll be sucking a lot of fugghan dust at the arse end of the column."

In Texas, Marlow had learned that Indians did not move easily, or without a fight, especially when prodded by the Army and their weapons. Even though they were unarmed, Marlow could imagine the Indians making trouble among themselves or for the Army. In either case, Marlow knew it meant bloodshed. *Shit*, Marlow said to himself. *I volunteered to see the world, not to fight a bunch of wild Indians.*

O'Riley spat a wad of tobacco from his mouth and continued. "There'll be almost a thousand Ute ponies, plus our three-hundred replacements and the teamsters' spare mules. If any animal falls behind, including Indian ponies and sheep, and *they* can't be easily returned to the main column . . . just let 'em go. You're not being paid to recover livestock, except for our own remounts."

Soldiers hunched their shoulders in response to the cold wind blowing in from the mountains to the south. Several whispered to each other before the sergeant shouted, "*At ease!*" Then O'Riley turned to Private Bailey, known by all as the company fuckup, the soldier who always lost his equipment, turned up late for inspections, and was never in the right place in a formation. "Bailey, what brand do our remounts carry?"

Long silence. "Bailey, did you hear me?"

"Yeah, Sarge. I'm thinking."

"Well think faster, you dumb-arse."

More silence. Then Bailey blurted out, "US."

"And where is the brand located on the horse?"

Bailey looked over at a nearby hitching post where two horses were tied.

"Left side, Sarge," Bailey said.

"Where on the left side, you bloody idiot?"

"High up."

"I'll put this riding crop high up your arse," the sergeant said, "if you can't be more specific."

Marlow, who stood next to Bailey, whispered, "Shoulder."

"On the left shoulder, Sarge."

"Bailey, I have to admit that you're one smart somma bitch today. What you been eating?"

"Civilian food."

Laughter and cheers roared through the company ranks.

"*At ease!*" O'Riley shouted.

Silence returned, but the grins endured.

O'Riley continued. "We don't know what trouble to expect, but be prepared to chase down anyone who tries to escape. Shavano is their new chief after Ouray died last year. No one knows if he has the same control over his young bucks as Ouray. But if any Indian tries to escape, just shoot to kill the red bastard and don't fugghan forget the colonel has ordered 'no prisoners.' Again, I repeat: *no prisoners.*

"In preparation for tomorrow's march, today will be given over to mounted target practice, horse care, and the repair and cleaning of equipment. I want your arses properly dressed and mounted in formation by seven fifteen. You have one hour to grab breakfast, get to the armory for your weapons and ammo, saddle up, and fall into formation behind the company guidon." O'Riley pointed to the swallow-tailed red-and-white guidon flag designating Company C.

"If you can't remember what unit this is, ask Private Fuckup."

Some muffled laughter drifted through the ranks before O'Riley ordered, "*Company dismissed.*"

Colonel Joseph Kindred, the regiment's commanding officer—often referred to by his troops as "the biggest toad in the puddle"—walked by the formation as the soldiers scattered to their temporary barracks. He carried himself straight-backed but with a slight limp. On his right hand he wore a white leather glove to cover the three fingers he'd lost in the Civil War. His penetrating dark-brown eyes never wandered from the subject of his attention, and his dark, droopy cavalry mustache only accentuated his dour countenance. When he did smile, it usually resulted from an act of unusual cruelty he himself had devised for use against an Indian opponent.

O'Riley saluted the colonel as he approached.

As Kindred's gloved right hand moved to return the recognition from the sergeant, it looked more like a pigeon in flight than a proper military salute.

"Are they ready to move these red niggers, Sergeant?" the colonel asked O'Riley.

"Yes, sir," he responded.

"Your company needs to be prepared for trouble. Have your troopers ride with their carbines locked and loaded, same for their pistols . . . and sabers sharpened."

"Sir, may I suggest we leave our sabers behind? They get in the bloody way when we're reloading our carbines or pistols on horseback."

"Sergeant, your company is a cavalry outfit. Correct? This regiment, a specially assembled combined infantry and cavalry unit, is a marriage of firepower and mobility. And that includes sabers. Your troops *will* ride with sabers."

"Yes, sir," O'Riley said as he snapped to attention.

After the company sergeant's inspection and announcements, Kindred met with senior staff and company commanders within earshot of the troops. "As we move these Ute, we are under orders to 'protect them.' But I want you to know my orders also authorize me to use whatever force is necessary to accomplish the Ute removal. I want all individual weapons, including the Gatling guns, inspected by company sergeants before taps." Kindred hesitated and then added, "If we need to use torture to get them to move their red asses, we will."

Marlow thought, *I wonder what new cruelty the colonel has invented for this mission.*

Kindred continued. "I will not allow my troops to be outgunned like the cavalry up on the White River two years ago. Nor will what happened to General Custer and his troopers five years ago in Montana be repeated. If we're forced by the Ute to use our combined firepower, and I personally hope we *will* have that opportunity, we will make amends for Custer's death."

Mention of Custer caught the attention of the officers, who nodded their approval at the thought of revenge. Kindred almost smiled.

"The Colorado newspapers declared: THE UTES MUST GO. Well, by God, they're going! We'll push them in front of our weapons into Utah, where the damned Mormons can deal with them. They deserve each other, as far as I'm concerned."

The officers broke from the meeting. A young lieutenant turned to an older officer and commented, "I heard this colonel to be one ornery son of a bitch."

"I served with him in Texas; you've not seen the worst of him yet."

*   *   *

By midafternoon, after a day of practicing horse maneuvers, firing weapons, and caring for their mounts, Marlow and Dolan sat outside their squad tent on log stools cleaning their weapons.

"Marlow, tell me why this fucking Army has us go through a bunch of worthless maneuvers that, as we all know, have no useful purpose against the redskins? You don't see the Indians using double columns, countermarching, or facing formations. They don't wheel into double columns to attack us. Hell no, they use their most effective maneuver—the ambush—even at night. In daylight, they wait until we're in the open and then they attack, charging us from behind boulders. Or they wait until we're stuck in some isolated fucking canyon without any escape route and then pounce on us like a mountain lion on a deer. And all we can do is trot around in formations designed by Europeans while a trumpet announces our arrival to the enemy."

Dolan yanked the cleaning rod from the barrel of his carbine as he spit a wad of tobacco to the ground. He shook his head at his bunkmate. "Hiram, we're wasting our fucking time. You ever see a cavalry regiment sneak up on an Indian encampment?"

"Well, what about Custer?" Marlow answered.

"Yeah, and look what happened to that dumb-ass general. But I'm bored as hell sitting around waiting for nothing to happen," Dolan complained.

"Me too. But far better to be working our horses than taking arrows to the chest. From what the sarge says, we can probably expect to see some arrows."

Dolan didn't want to hear about what the sarge had to say. It was always bad news. For the time being, he'd rather learn more about his bunkmate. But like all troopers he didn't want to get too personal. Many soldiers had enlisted to avoid bad debts, a bad marriage, or a jail sentence, the kind of things best left behind and unspoken. "How in hell did your ass end up here from Iowa, Marlow? Isn't that where you from?" Geography mattered to soldiers, especially for those who carried a bias against Southerners.

"Iowa's right. I needed to get out from under my father's thumb on the family farm. I only stayed as long as I did after high school to help my brother, Sam, and my father, who was injured in the War. The farm always seemed shorthanded, even after we hired a young Dakota Sioux Indian. To me, thirteen dollars a month, a three-year enlistment, and the opportunity to see something other than an Iowa cornfield sounded like a better life than dragging my ass behind a plow in the rain or slopping pigs in the muck. Now I'm not so certain."

"Where were you posted before here?" Dolan asked.

"In 1875, after I enlisted in Kansas City, they sent me to the cavalry center at Fort Riley. You trained there too, right? I learned the basic trooper skills—riding in those dumb fucking formations, and how to use the saber, pistol, and carbine. I already knew how to train and care for the animals. My experience with farm horses helped get me corporal stripes, but the promotion also meant a transfer to Fort Union in the New Mexico Territory. That place is about as close to hell as you ever want to get."

"Hot as hell, I hear," Dolan said.

"As a member of C Company, 4th Cavalry Regiment, under Colonel Kindred, I spent a long year guarding supply caravans and immigrant trains moving through Comanche territory on the Santa Fe Trail. Kindred is a hard-ass commander, and that was damned unpleasant duty. I saw what a Comanche raiding party could do to an emigrant wagon train. Mean sons of bitches, those Comanche. They'd kill all the emigrants, scalp them, mutilate their bodies . . . whole families slaughtered."

Dolan interrupted. "Did they have guns?"

"Damned right they did. And they knew how to use 'em. We all feared the Comanche more than any other tribe. Like some other soldiers I know, I'd put my pistol to my head before I let a Comanche capture me.

"Let me tell you, the Ute we're guarding here are peaceful angels compared to the Comanche. Our interpreter, Mr. Carroll, tells me the Ute call the Comanche the 'people who fight all the time.' On my last tour with Kindred, we encountered a large band of Comanche led by Chief Quanah Parker in the Palo Duro Canyon. The colonel ordered us to kill every one of the sons of bitches—men, women, and children . . . and their horses."

Dolan stared at Marlow as he continued. "We didn't kill Parker because the Army wanted him brought to Fort Sill alive, probably because the senior officer wanted the pleasure of watching him hang.

"I've been here at the Uncompahgre Cantonment since early this year . . . a nice change from the Texas heat and the Comanche arrows. Now here I am with you to guard these Ute and, until now, keep them peacefully corralled in this outside reservation pen. I don't know about you, but I've never encountered any problem with them. It's the white traders from Ouray who stir up trouble when they sneak from town onto the reservation to trade weapons and liquor for hides."

Dolan volunteered, "Talk about Ouray: Sarge told me we lost three more deserters the other night. Never came back from town. Probably got stuck rutting in a hog farm. I hear we're missing twenty percent of the regiment to desertion and almost as many down with scurvy, dysentery, or the clap. Sarge says we'll be real shorthanded on the move to Utah. Those hog farms in Ouray sure need to clean themselves up. But to be honest, I could use one more trip into town for some snatch."

"Watch yourself, Dolan. Remember the colonel ranting about all those dirty doves in Ouray and not havin' any docs here to treat us. Thank God I'm clean. Are you?"

"As clean as a teenage virgin. Lucky, I guess," Dolan said with a smirk.

"All I want is to get through my enlistment alive, with my scalp, my health, and maybe a little money in my pocket." Marlow sighed. "As I see it, the problem for us peons is that our officers are looking for a good fight with *any* Indians we encounter, even those carrying a white flag. Look what happened at Sand Creek when the Arapahoe waved a white flag before the Army."

Marlow ran his hand slowly over the polished wood of his carbine. "The Army starts the fight, the Indians get murdered, and the officers get promoted. No other way for them to get ahead these days, except maybe marry a general's daughter or have a friend in Congress. You can bet our toad is looking for a good fight if it's the only way for that SOB to replace the eagle on his shoulder with a star. We're Kindred's cannon fodder for that star. If we end up KIA, it'll be because of his fucking ambition. 'Bout the only thing we can do is stay healthy. How's your health, Dolan?"

"Good, except for them hemorrhoids from my saddle, that ball-busting piece of shit General McClellan left us."

"You need to pack the center slot of a McClellan saddle with an extra shirt, or some horsehair," Marlow advised. "That'll keep your balls from being squashed."

"Wish to hell we had a doctor to treat us. I won't miss this shithole. But Utah will probably be worse."

"Maybe, but remember, we're coming right back here after we dump the Utes into Mormon country."

"By the time we get back here, if I'm still alive, my enlistment is up."

"Mine too," Marlow replied with a smile.

The skies darkened as taps blew. The men wiped their weapons clean of solvent and placed them at the head of their bedrolls. Marlow poured a cup of water from his polished canteen and fell asleep thinking about the next day's move.

★   ★   ★

The next morning at formation, O'Riley announced some unexpected news.

"Last night Shavano came to the colonel in the early morning hours to say that some of his young warriors refused to go to Utah. The colonel shared with the company sergeants what he told Shavano through the interpreter, Mr. Carroll: 'I don't give a rat's ass what your young warriors think about the move. You tell them they have two hours to make a decision. They can either agree to move or stay. If they decide to remain here, they will be captured and shot before your entire band at seven this morning.' Our Gatling guns appearing on the flanks of the Ute encampment this morning may have changed their minds. We'll see.

"When we move out, we'll take our position, you'll be happy to know, at the tail end, where you can suck all the dust you want. The colonel says we can expect to be on the trail a little over three weeks, maybe less, depending on the weather and Indian behavior. After we break from formation, pick up your three-day rations, twenty-five carbine cartridges, and twenty pistol rounds. You will, on the colonel's orders, ride with sabers."

A long moan could be heard throughout the company.

"*At ease!*" O'Riley shouted. "After gathering your gear, piss on your fires and mount up. You are to be in formation at sunrise. Dismissed."

Marlow hoped Shavano could maintain discipline among his younger braves. The Indian agent, Mr. Baxter, said he would. Given their comments, Marlow doubted that O'Riley, the colonel, and his senior staff would agree.

TWO

ON THE MARCH, WESTERN COLORADO
September 1881

Marlow was pleased to be leaving the Uncompahgre Cantonment and the daily routine of an Army post. As much as he enjoyed Colorado's cooler fall weather, he, like all soldiers, complained about the boredom of garrison life. With his horse skills, he hadn't enlisted to build corrals, storage sheds, a jail/guardhouse, or patch adobe buildings with mud and straw. He dreaded guard duty and the loss of a night's sleep. Anything in the field surpassed maintenance chores. Even the chopping and hauling firewood from the nearby forest served as a welcome relief.

On alternate days Marlow trained his two three-year-old geldings. His favorite, Chunk, so named because of his muscle pattern, Marlow had selected from thirty new remounts delivered to the company in midsummer. Marlow pleaded with O'Riley to have the horse assigned to him. A bottle of cheap brandy consummated the deal. He worked the horses slowly and with patience, never forcing them into unfamiliar routines. He taught them to change leads, moving in stages from a fast walk to a dogtrot to a fast gallop. He trained them to cross streams and rivers in a heavy current, move through mud and sand and over rocky bottoms. He had them walk blindfolded through timber with only the rider's guidance and then stand motionless as he fired his carbine over their heads. On steep, rocky hillsides, he accustomed them to be mounted and dismounted from either side and, on command, to lie flat on the ground while Marlow steadied his carbine on the horses' ribs and fired off two thunderous shots. To improve their stamina, he rode his horses hard.

The most difficult skill he practiced repeatedly. With his horse in a full gallop, he dropped his reins over the horse's neck, steered the horse with leg pressure or a gentle poke of a spur, removed his carbine from his shoulder sling, and fired over the horse's head at a stationary target. Only about one in five troopers possessed the riding skill to steady a carbine on a galloping horse and fire off a well-aimed shot. When the target became a mounted and armed Indian, a well-aimed shot became more difficult. In the heat of battle, troopers too often hit the back of their own horse's head rather than an Indian or his pony thirty yards away. That might have been why a regimental infantry sergeant said he had no use for the cavalry and its inept firepower. "If you'd get off those goddamned rocking horses of yours, maybe you'd kill some Indians. You'd be far better off eating 'em than riding 'em."

But not Marlow's horses. Always trained to perfection, in superb flesh, feet trimmed and manes combed or braided, his horses were the envy of every trooper in the company. It took him three months to train each of his two horses. By autumn, he, with each of his mounts, had created a beautifully coordinated team. Marlow took great pleasure in his equine accomplishments, their day-to-day progress, and their self-confidence with newly acquired skills. That Marlow also earned additional cash from other troopers when they asked him to help with their green mounts only added to his pleasure.

★   ★   ★

After the soldiers received their last instructions from O'Riley at the early morning formation, they moved to the picket line to find their mounts. Even in the poor light, they identified their individual horses by a recognizable mark—a white star on the forehead, two white socks, a uniquely trimmed mane or tail, or, in the case of Private Bailey's horse, a pink ribbon twisted in its black mane.

"Bailey, why the fugghan pink ribbon?" Sergeant O'Riley asked.

"A way to identify him in the dark, Sarge."

"Listen up, soldier. We're not goin' to a fugghan English horse show, you bloody fool. I suppose you sprayed him with perfume so he'd smell good for the judges? Cut that ribbon off, Bailey, and tie it to your cap. That way I can keep an eye on you." Then O'Riley added, "You'll also make a better target for the redskins."

"You want me dead, Sarge?"

"Only if I can't get you reassigned to a different company."

The soldiers checked their horses' shoes, many of which had been changed or reset the night before; exchanged bridles for halters; rechecked their saddle cinches for tightness; and swung up onto the cold backs of horses, where they set themselves in the uncomfortable, one-size-fits-none saddles. They secured their sabers, snapped the guard straps over their holstered pistols, and slung their carbines over their shoulders. A few troopers, like Marlow, brought their own saddles to the Army to avoid the discomfort of the cavalry's McClellan model. As the troopers moved into formation, one young enlistee riding next to Marlow asked, "I hear we won't run into any Comanche, but these Ute, are they as cruel and vicious as the Comanche? I want to return home with my scalp."

"You've got nothing to fear," Marlow responded. "Probably no Comanche between here and Utah, and as long as we don't aggravate the Ute, we'll be fine. In the future, you might cut your hair real short like mine. Makes it more difficult for the Indians to scalp you."

"I'll shave my head tonight," the new recruit said.

Marlow laughed and reminded the trooper, "Shaved heads are not allowed by the Army, a regulation written by Washington generals who never fought Indians."

Captain John Griffin, the C Company commander, rode forward to say, "The colonel wants us to keep civilians at a good distance from the troops and the Indians. Immediately after we remove the Ute, the civilians from the town of Ouray will want to stake claims on the Ute's vacated reservation land. Already two Ouray residents have been chased off. Do the same if you encounter any."

Nothing I can't handle, Marlow said to himself.

While the troops waited for the signal to move out in the gray light of dawn, Marlow watched the white smoke rise from the Indian lodges, where the Ute killed their fires, disassembled their teepees, and loaded their travois, stretcher-like conveyances dragged behind a horse or dog. Only the nickering of horses and the barking of their mongrel dogs broke the morning stillness.

Just at sunrise, under a clear sky, Chief Shavano sent a messenger to Kindred reporting that his band was ready to move. On the colonel's command, cavalry horses galloped to the front of the Indian column while the infantry wagons with cavalry escorts moved to the flanks. As the column moved west into drier, dusty landscape, Marlow thought back on the attractive Uncompahgre Valley and how he made friends with a few of the Ute now to his front.

On Sundays, his one free day, he rode his youngest three-year-old colt out into the valley and through the Indians' lodges. Marlow never felt any threat from the Ute. Troopers at the cantonment who had more experience with the Indians than Marlow always thought of the Ute as a peace-loving tribe, except when challenged by other tribes for their hunting grounds, or when, on occasion, they were treated unfairly by a cruel and incompetent Indian agent.

Marlow became a familiar sight riding among the lodges on Sundays. He was invited into numerous homes, all smelling of smoke and food, where he was welcomed with a piece of fresh-baked bread topped with sweet nut paste. At one lodge, a short, stocky, middle-aged brave invited Marlow to ride out into the valley to show off his most valued assets—four ponies in perfect flesh, heavily muscled, with stout legs and hard feet. Marlow offered two bags of coffee for the largest pony, but no trade could be struck. When they returned to the lodge, Marlow noticed four braided horsehair bridles hanging on a peg. He picked up one, indicated to the brave its beauty, and handed him two bags of coffee. The brave shook his head and raised three fingers, and Marlow nodded. The next

Sunday he returned with the coffee in exchange for the bridle with its colorful designs. The trade culminated with an offering of more warm bread with nut paste and sweetened hot coffee.

Every Sunday Marlow visited the brave and his family. He played with the children, who ran around the lodge wearing Marlow's campaign hat, and familiarized himself with some Ute words and phrases. He learned the basic skills of tanning a hide and braiding horsehair. Other Ute rode to the lodge to get a close-up look at a cavalry trooper. They offered him food and a pipe while conversing in sign language. Marlow came to understand sign language well enough to learn that no Ute wanted to move to Utah. Could he stop it? No, he responded, he had no power to change the mind of the White Father in Washington. They continued, however, to enjoy each other's presence.

Marlow had no quarrel with the Ute, or any other Indian tribe for that matter, except for the Comanche. As the march got under way, Marlow asked himself if Kindred would treat the Ute differently than the dreaded Comanche. From what Marlow learned from fellow troopers who had served with Kindred, and from Marlow's own experience, he thought not. The company, as ordered, fell in behind the Indians and their remuda.

★   ★   ★

Most soldiers had altered the uncomfortable blue cavalry wool riding trousers by reinforcing the insides of the knees and seats with a layer of sheepskin or deer hide. On their saddles the troopers carried blanket rolls, tent halves, overcoats with spare clothing rolled inside, and lariats and picket pins strapped on top. They also brought along brush and shoe pouches, forage sacks with oats and corn, saddle-bags with personal belongings, and haversacks containing rations—hardtack, bacon, coffee—slung over one of the saddlebags. Canteens and mugs, supplemented often with cooking kettles, pots, skillets, and other camping gear, completed their baggage. The troopers had punched into their cartridge belts their supply of ammunition for their single-shot, breech-loading Springfield carbines. When a cavalry company moved in column, it sounded like the inside of a hardware store in an earthquake.

The clanking pots and pans from the soldier's haver-sacks were enough to alert the remuda that C Company had ridden in behind them. With a few hollers from the soldiers, the horses followed the Indian column. Marlow could see a few civilian riders who had already assembled to the south along a split-rail fence, waiting to rush into the heart of the vacated reservation to stake their claims.

What a beautiful lush valley we're leaving, Marlow thought. *If I were a Ute, I wouldn't want to leave either. Maybe when my enlistment is up in two months, I might stake a claim here myself.*

Yells from fellow troopers interrupted Marlow's thoughts. He turned in his saddle as a civilian intruder rode up on Marlow's right side and passed at a fast gallop. Marlow chased after him. Within twenty seconds Marlow had hold of the rider's reins close to the bit, pulling the panting horse to a stop.

"And where are you off to in such a hurry, mister?" Marlow asked.

"Get your goddamned hands off my reins," the intruder said.

A rough-looking sort, Marlow thought, not well mounted, and dressed in the filthy clothes of a miner.

"I don't have to answer to no horse bugger."

Marlow saw the handle of a pistol sticking out from the rider's belt. Almost on reflex, Marlow dropped his reins from his right hand, pulled his leather quirt from under his cartridge belt, and, with the quickness of a boxer, backhanded the quirt's rawhide laces across the rider's eyes. Then Marlow slid across his saddle, grabbed the rider in a bear hug, and pulled him to the ground. He jammed the tip of his right spur into the man's back. Dolan appeared at the wrestling match with his pistol drawn.

"Get your ass off the ground," Dolan shouted at the civilian. "Drop that pistol and kick it toward me, hands over your head. One unexpected shiver or shake, and I'll show you what a forty-five-caliber bullet can do to your chest."

The man nodded, stood, withdrew the small pistol from his belt, dropped it, and kicked the weapon away.

"Now look here, fellows. I'm only wantin' to put a claim on dat quarter section of grass right over dere. Folks in town said we could stake a claim right after dem Indians moved out, and see, dey've moved," the man said as he pointed west.

"I don't know who in hell said you could move in right behind, but he's full of shit. Mount up. We're going to see the company commander. Any more trouble from you, buster, and you'll be human fertilizer for your grass plot." Marlow picked up the pistol and tied the intruder's hands behind his back with rawhide straps.

The two soldiers accompanied the captured miner to Captain Griffin. "And what have we here," the captain asked, "a volunteer for the US Army?"

"No, sir," Marlow responded. "You wouldn't want this piece of shit in the Army. I caught him trying to stake a claim—had a loaded pistol in his belt, and said it was OK to come on the reservation immediately after the Ute left."

"What's your name, mister, and where you from?" the captain asked.

"Horst Meyer. I'm from Ouray, a miner."

"Corporal, take Mr. Meyer back to the cantonment and have him placed in the guardhouse. Meyer, you're under arrest for unauthorized entry to an Indian reservation. Marlow, tell the guard it's minimum rations for Mr. Meyer. I'll deal with him when we get back from Utah."

As the column of Indians and their military escort moved west, Marlow took the reins of the prisoner's horse. "Better hold on with your knees, Meyer, 'cause we're off to the races."

Back at the cantonment, Marlow shoved Meyer off his horse and handed the prisoner over to the armed guards and then rode off at a hard gallop to catch up with his company, which had been joined by the regiment's Indian interpreter, Ben Carroll. Carroll rode a wooden saddle covered with a blanket on an Appaloosa pony with its tail tied up and guided by a jaw rein. He possessed the features of his Ute mother—high cheekbones, cinnamon-colored skin, a short stocky body, and braided black hair tied off with piece of red ribbon—and the deep-blue eyes of his American father. Carroll greeted Marlow as he joined him in the column. "Glad you join us today on this lovely picnic, Hiram." The soldiers who depended upon Carroll's "interpreter English" recognized his proficiency with adjectives but his difficulty with verb tenses and articles.

"Wouldn't have missed this fun or your company for anything," Marlow responded with a smile and asked Carroll if he had brought his deck of cards. Marlow could never figure how in hell a half-breed could make so much money at the cantonment's Friday night poker games. It was over cards that Marlow first learned something about Carroll's background.

He'd been born on the reservation, a day's ride to the northeast from the Uncompahgre Indian Agency. His father, a trapper born in Wisconsin, had married an Uncompahgre Ute and lived in the valley until he'd had an argument with one of Chief Ouray's sub-chiefs about hunting rights.

Riding with the interpreter, Marlow asked Carroll more about his boyhood.

"My father, mother's family, and three other braves and their families moved away from Ouray's band, forty-five miles to the northeast, still reservation land. There, I born. At age of fifteen, my father leave on hunting trip. He never returned. After, I lived with my mother, aunts, cousins, and grandmother. We all remain members of Uncompahgre band and come down to agency each month for rations. Our names is in the Uncompahgre census."

As the two men rode side by side, their eyes focused on the remuda directly to their front. Marlow described to Carroll the small ruckus caused by the intruder and then asked, "I'm curious, Ben. Why did some young braves refuse to leave this area and threaten a fight before Kindred threatened to put them before a firing squad?"

Carroll said, "You must learn this area in western and southern Colorado, land and most of Utah Territory, is ancestral home to us for two or three centuries past. There are no evil spirits here anymore. We removed them. Forests, meadows, rivers, and wildlife give us life here where we are safe. The land is sacred to us. It give our forefathers life, and if we care for land, it give us life now, and life for our children in future. Our tribal history is in this land. We know every feature of it, location of wild-life, water springs, wild fruit, plants to heal, and healthy grass for our horses. Remains of ancestors are spread over this area. Many moons ago, Ute accepted responsibility to care for land for our creator and for our children. This is our home forever, say three treaties signed by two White Fathers in Washington."

"So what happened to the promise?"

"That massacre up on White River two years ago and killing of Agent Meeker changed everything. I think Washington send Meeker to White River agency to stir up trouble with Ute. When Agent Meeker asked for Army help to arrest two innocent Ute, Army come onto reserva-tion. We tell Army they have no right to come on reserva-tion. They come anyway. Then Indians kill agency white workers and take white women and children hostage. Ute also killed many Army soldiers and commanding officer. In treaty that end fighting, Washington punish us and take away our Colorado reservation . . . sixteen million acres. In return we get about a million acres in Utah and another million acres of sagebrush down on New Mexico border. We no understand why the government thieves who steal our land are not punished. If Ute steal, often he is killed by tribe. You whites take land from Indians. Maybe tomor-row someone take it from you. Then what you do?"

"You sure were messed over by the government," Marlow responded.

"What mean 'messed over'?" Carroll asked

"The Ute, like other tribes, have been treated real bad. That's what it means."

"That for certain. I know is not first time and probably not last. Even those who say they are our friend turn out be our enemy. You know that bigwig trader Otto Mears? He calls himself friend of Chief Ouray. For years he fills his pockets with money given him by Indian agency for our rations. You not survive three days on rotten rations he supply us. And that one-armed Army major, the one who go down Colorado River through Grand Canyon, Powell I think his name, another false friend of Ute. He tell Indian Commission in Washington that if White Father wants to punish and destroy Ute for killing Agent Meeker and soldiers at White River, the government must take our ancestral land."

Carroll halted his horse and took a small plug of tobacco from his saddlebag. He took a bite, offered the plug to Marlow, who refused it, and continued. "Many Americans think our land free and open for homestead. But this land taken from Indians, and not just Ute land. Many Americans not see Indians they are stealing from; and if they not know them, or since they be a different color, it really not stealing. In treaties, new white-man laws not mention the word 'steal.' Much use of word 'protect' for white land taken from Indian. But that is what United States do for long time. They steal our land and put Ute in outside pens, what you call reservation. Now Washington steals reservation and puts us in smaller box. Ancestors tell us white man's diseases kill off many Indians all over country, not Army bullets and sabers. With more braves Indians could better defend their land against homesteaders and Army."

Marlow felt ignorant to respond, except to offer advice. "You Ute are wise not to fight the Army. They're looking for an excuse to fight you, and in a battle they could kill most of your braves in a day. Remember what Kindred did to the Comanche. But I do understand your reaction to the broken promises of Washington. Not a good situation."

Marlow asked, "Ben, how'd you come to be an interpreter here for the Army?" Before Carroll answered, the two men reined their horses to a stop and watched a Ute family pull out from the column with a broken travois. Ben and Marlow had their own problems to contend with and couldn't render assistance and stay in a position to keep the Indian ponies from escaping the remuda. The Ute squaw dismounted, reattached one of the drag poles to the travois, screamed at and kicked the pulling pony, and remounted. The men returned their attention to conversation.

"One ration day, three years ago, the former agent here, Mr. Coddington, know I speak fair English, and write some also. These skills I learned from my father."

"And poker, also?"

Carroll smiled and continued. "Coddington asked if I like to interpret for extra rations. To help feed my family, I say yes. The new agent, Mr. Baxter, asked me to stay when agency moved here to Uncompahgre Valley. Good thing Washington changed agents, or Ute kill him, like they do to Agent Meeker. We hate Coddington. He play favorites and withhold rations to punish us. I also know he give rations to his brother-in-law, who he hired as agency carpenter. The brother-in-law take rations into Ouray and sell them to the miners for much money. Chief Ouray complained to the governor, who passed word to Washington about corrupt Coddington. Finally, we get new agent."

As the two men rode along through sage flats at the end of the half-mile column, Marlow pulled the yellow bandanna from his neck and splashed water on it from his canteen. He wrapped the wet cloth around his face and across his nose to filter the dust.

Carroll continued, "Not a bad life as interpreter, but I not see my mother and cousins very often. I read much to help my English. But it is tough business, dangerous also. For example, the treaties your government presented to us these past years include many new words invented by white lawyers. I not certain after rereading treaty we signed eight years ago, when we sell San Juan mining district, that I understand all provisions. Money go into trust, they tell us, to benefit Ute in future. What is trust, a kind of bank?"

"I'm not certain."

"We never see money. Must we hope that it is still there? Also as interpreter, I learned it is best not to give a word-for-word translation. You know what I mean?"

"I can understand, especially when you're dealing with Kindred. From what I've seen of the colonel, he's not the most diplomatic officer. He's got a foul mouth and a temper."

"That is true. For example, when Colonel Kindred called Chief Shavano 'dumb son of a bitch' in his face a couple of days ago, I substituted word 'unfriendly.' I left out 'son of a bitch' part because it translates 'son of a whore' . . . very bad term in Ute. I know I prevented big fight. That colonel of yours, big temper, he cause some trouble for us before we get to Utah. You wait and see."

"He sure as hell caused me some trouble with the Comanche in Texas. Tough job you took on, Ben."

As they rode on together, Carroll continued to offer stories about his people and the land they were leaving behind. Marlow came to learn more about Ute life, their winter migration to the warmer climate and grass of the

Grand Valley, the locations of their summer and fall hunting grounds in and around the Uncompahgre Valley, their trade of horses and hides with other Ute bands and tribes and at their visits to the trade fairs in Taos and Santa Fe.

Carroll went on to explain the Utes' fear of the US Army. "They always make trouble in this area—or any area. As you and I know, the only way to get promotion, with War ended, is start fight with Indians and then blow their heads off. I know Kindred loves this assignment here. The more Indians he kills, the faster he gets to be general."

"Ben, you have the Army and the colonel figured out real good."

"I know Kindred background real good," Carroll responded.

Marlow too knew something of Kindred from his service with him in Texas. Marlow told Carroll, "Kindred is a strict, by-the-book commander who always needs to demonstrate his authority, lest it be challenged by a junior officer or, God forbid, a lowly soldier. In Texas, we troopers feared Kindred more than we respected him. We called him the 'Perpetual Punisher,' because of the cruel punishments he inflicted on badly behaved enlisted men and the occasional junior officer who failed in his responsibilities. Hauling a log, hanging by the thumbs, spread eagle on a wheel, and getting dunked in a water tank were his ideas of discipline."

Marlow went on about Kindred as he rode side by side with Carroll. "I heard Kindred was a brave commander on Civil War battlefields, including Antietam, Gettysburg, and Petersburg. He suffered wounds to his leg, shoulder, chest, and hand. Despite the injuries, he never left the battlefield. But for all of his bravery, he has an impulsive and vicious personality, like a badger: overly fierce, wild, and maybe too aggressive for his own good."

"Sounds a little like Custer," Carroll said.

"Probably so," Marlow responded. "I think they were at West Point together.

Marlow went on to talk about an Ouray newspaper article that appeared when Kindred transferred to the Uncompahgre Cantonment. The paper quoted General Ulysses Grant, who, after the Civil War, called Kindred "the most promising young officer in the Army." Kindred had further advanced his reputation in the 1870s, particularly with Generals Grant and Sherman, when he led the 4th Cavalry Regiment in successful engagements against the Comanche, Kiowa, Apache, and Kickapoo in Texas and the Cheyenne in the Black Hills. "General Sheridan said that Kindred is a seasoned and successful Indian fighter. The brass just loves him. That's why Kindred is here and we're unlucky enough to be under his command."

Carroll nodded. "Friends in high places."

"There's something else I remember about that newspaper article. Not everyone is a fan of the colonel. In a Civil War battle where Kindred commanded a unit of Connecticut volunteers, one officer under his command, who became a US senator, referenced Kindred's cruel personality and volcanic temper.

"After the Connecticut unit suffered a seventy percent casualty rate, the senator blamed Kindred's poor leadership. Kindred further pissed off the senator when he took full credit for the hard-won victory."

"I can tell you, Hiram, Indians call the colonel 'Bad Hand' or 'No Finger Chief,' and fear him more than any other Army officer. He burns all Indian camps he sees, and kills every Indian on sight, no matter it be a warrior, squaw, or baby. The ponies the colonel not take . . . all shot . . . Same with buffalo. Big waste."

Carroll changed the subject to the Ute as the column moved slowly but steadily west. "We Ute commit no crimes and follow agreements we signed in 1868 and 1873 with your presidents in Washington. They break agreements and treaties we signed in good faith. They cut rations, send corrupt agents, and put money from land sales in hidden trust run by thieves. We know the cost of new buildings, seed, farm implements, and livestock come from trust. We see no account of money."

After a long silence, Marlow asked, "Ben, what makes a good chief like Chief Ouray?"

"A good chief, everyone listens to him and obey what he says. If Ouray alive today, we no go to Utah. Shavano is not good chief . . . much different from Ouray."

"What do the Ute want in their chief?" Marlow asked.

"He must be good hunter, know when and where to hunt. He must be brave in battle; also wise about who to fight and when. Chief must be fair in treatment of other Ute, listen carefully, and never lose temper. Most important, Chief must know tribal history from very beginning to present time and know how to tell it to tribe. Ouray do that. Your White Fathers in Washington, they know your history and teach it to all Americans?"

To avoid a long discussion about leadership qualities, Marlow said, "White Fathers have some of the same traits." He wanted to add, "but few of our military leaders do."

Carroll looked for an excuse to break from the discussion. "I need to find the colonel. He probably search for me. Always need help to fire his cigar. I see he know only way to be Army chief is to act like mean son of a bitch."

"Take care, Ben. Say hello to the colonel for all of us back here sucking dust, and don't lose those cards. See you in Utah," Marlow said as Carroll trotted off to the head of the column.

The column of Indians and their guards moved slowly but without incident. By the end of four days they had traveled almost one hundred miles to the junction of the Uncompahgre and the Gunnison Rivers. This was a better-than-average distance by Army standards, especially for a contingent of more than 1,500 Indians, 250 mounted soldiers, plus 18 wagons carrying supplies, 480 infantrymen, and almost 1,300 trailing horses. Kindred pushed them hard.

As the sun melted into the darkening western sky, the Indians and troopers made their separate camps at the rivers' confluence, where they found ample grass for horses. The dark rain clouds and lightning to the east encouraged the soldiers to pitch two-man tents, while only a few Indian families bothered to put up their tepees. The Indians and soldiers in separate search parties scoured the river's high-water mark for driftwood and dried willows. Within an hour, all had cook fires going. A couple of troopers, aided by live grasshoppers, hooked some rainbows, a welcome supplement to the dried beans, salted meat, and cornbread the cooks offered for supper. Sergeant O'Riley pulled a dented canteen from his saddlebag and poured whiskey into his coffee. He made no offer to share the popular commodity.

Before taps, soldiers sat before their fires, patching their uniforms, mending a bridle or a set of reins, and cleaning weapons. Marlow demonstrated to new recruits how to file the firing mechanism on a carbine to allow for a quicker shot with a hair trigger. "Now you're ready to take on some redskins," Marlow said to an eighteen-year-old German recruit who spoke little English.

That night Sergeant O'Riley informed his troopers that they'd be crossing the Colorado River the next day. "If your horse stumbles and goes down, forget your gear . . . just swim to the nearest shore. If you can't swim, grab your horse's tail. He'll pull you along. Some of you have horses that can ride double. So be alert to see who needs help, like Bailey. Bailey, do you swim?"

"No, Sarge."

"Hang on then, Bailey, and bring some soap. I want you to smell like a lilac bush in springtime when you wash ashore. Enjoy the water."

THREE

Around noon the next day, the column readied itself to cross the river. The mid-September weather was cool and sunny. Large cottonwoods, their yellowed leaves flashing against a royal-blue sky, marked the boundaries of the gently flowing river. Pockets of white water signaled the presence of some large boulders that had peeled off the sides of the surrounding mesas.

Carroll approached the colonel and reported that a Ute sub-chief suggested an easier crossing two miles downstream from the confluence of the Gunnison River with the Colorado. "Chief tell me no boulders, a sandy bottom, and only few deep holes. Ute use crossing every year on way to and from winter grazing ground." A small detachment of troopers and teamsters inspected the spot and gave their approval.

Two cavalry companies made it across the river without incident. The Indians too crossed with no difficulty except for one travois that broke loose from a pony in the heavy current. The Army wagons, burdened with infantry troops and supplies, crossed next. When they reached midstream, the mules struggled to find a firm footing. Several wagons made it across without difficulty. Another wagon bogged down in the sand and broke its double tree attached to the wagon's tongue. With the break, the mules pulled free of the flooded wagon, leaving the soldiers chest high in water and swearing at the "fucking mules" and the "dumb-ass, incompetent" teamsters.

One wagon that had already made a successful crossing emptied itself of its cargo and returned to the river to pick up the soldiers and supplies from what looked like a canvas-covered barge. After the effective transfer, the abandoned wagon floated free downstream. One trooper galloped along the bank in pursuit of it, rode into the river, and managed to get a rope around the brake handle, but he couldn't hold the weight. He stared helplessly as the wagon floated toward Utah.

As Marlow watched, C Company waited on the riverbank for their turn to cross. The troopers, unaccustomed to crossing a major river, looked on in fear at the water circus. Soldiers asked each other if they could swim. "My brother taught me to dog-paddle one summer," one tried to reassure himself. Others tightened their horses' cinches and checked to see if all their equipment was secured properly on their saddles.

From across the river, C Company observed as two mounted Indian braves broke from the Ute ranks. Immediately, four mounted troopers sped off in pursuit of the renegade natives. One soldier fired over the Indians' heads. The braves refused to stop as the cavalry horses gained on them. Remembering their orders not to take prisoners, the soldiers fired off two more shots. The two Indians fell to the ground. One soldier rode up to one of the wounded Indians and with his pistol shot him in the back of the head. The other soldier repeated the same act with the second Indian. The soldiers tied the corpses to the ends of their lariats and dragged them to where Kindred had stationed himself to oversee the crossing. The soldiers saluted the colonel, who returned the salute with his silver-handled riding crop. "Bully for you, boys," Kindred said with a wide smile. Then he waved to the opposite shore for the troops to continue their crossing.

The C Company troopers were careful to wait for an empty spot in the river before attempting to cross. In the river's middle, two horses stumbled and lost their riders. The soldiers, burdened by their carbines and sabers, reached for their horses' tails. Others floundered in the water as they stripped off gear and weapons. One soldier screamed over the water's noise from a sandbar where he stood in knee-deep water. Nearby, three mounted Indian observers shouted and gave hand signals to swim, a skill unknown to most cavalry troopers. Two horses swam by without riders, only their heads visible in the white water.

O'Riley made it across on his horse with difficulty and, from the opposite shore, shouted and waved to his water-bound trooper. Upon seeing O'Riley, the isolated soldier sucked up his courage, strapped his carbine to his back, and dog-paddled furiously thirty feet to shore.

Suddenly, everyone heard loud shouts for help from Private Bailey, flailing away in the water. A Ute on a large Appaloosa rode into the river, caught Bailey by the collar of his blouse, and managed to lift him onto the back of the horse. The brave turned his horse in midstream and headed for the sandbar, where he deposited Bailey. Bailey stood there vomiting water, then looked up at his Ute savior, placed his hands together, and gurgled, "Thank you." The Ute acknowledged the gesture with a nod and a large smile.

Sergeant O'Riley summoned Marlow. "Your horse ride double?"

"Of course," Marlow said.

"Ride out there to the sandbar and see if you can pick up that piece of dog shit that resembles Bailey."

Within five minutes, Marlow had Bailey on the back of his horse, making their way toward shore, where O'Riley watched and waited. The sergeant barked at Bailey six inches from his nose. "Everyone makes it across the river safely except for you, you worthless ass-wipe! That Indian and Marlow should have let you drown. Now where in hell is your bloody mount?"

Mounted soldiers nearby overheard O'Riley's verbal blast at Bailey. One soldier said to another, "Private Fuckup has performed again."

Bailey looked around and recognized his bay gelding twenty yards downstream on the bank, shaking itself dry. Water drained from Bailey's empty scabbard, his saddlebags, and the barrel of the carbine, which he'd had slung around his shoulder.

"Where's your saber, Bailey?"

Seeing that it was missing from his saddle, Bailey tried some humor on the sergeant.

"Lost it, Sarge, spearing that killer whale in midstream."

"Oh, aren't we the smart-ass today? Bailey, if you don't get your fugghan act together by sundown, I'll put you up for a court-martial. Do I make myself clear? Now get over there, empty your boots, and get yourself mounted."

Bailey moved slowly down the sandy beach, water spilling from his trousers, blouse, and the tops of his boots. He sat on the riverbank and, with difficulty, pulled off his riding boots and emptied them onto the sand.

The sergeant looked over at Marlow. "Find that Indian rider who brought Bailey off the sandbar and bring him to me with the interpreter." Marlow wanted only to rest and dry off, but he followed O'Riley's order.

Within fifteen minutes, the interpreter and Bailey's Indian rescuer followed Marlow on horseback to where O'Riley, now joined by Captain Griffin, was sitting beneath a large cottonwood tree.

The captain noticed the Indian's muscular body, a large scar on his left forearm, a tattoo on his right forearm, and the beautiful beadwork on his wet deerskin shirt. The Indian rode with only a blanket covering his horse's back. Two polished brass buttons, which were attached to pieces of red ribbon, tied off his two long ebony braids.

Griffin looked at the Ute. "You saved the life of one of my troopers, and for that I am very grateful."

Carroll made the translation.

The captain reached into his wet saddlebag and pulled out a leather purse, opened it, and withdrew a small gold piece, along with a small wet sack of coffee beans. He handed both items to the Indian.

"What is your name?"

Carroll answered for the Indian. "Big Elk. We call him 'Elk' for short."

"You know this Indian?" the captain asked.

"Yes, sir, we grow up together on mesa near Los Piños Agency. Big Elk my cousin," the interpreter said.

Marlow noticed that both Indians had a tattoo of a bear's claw on their right forearms, a mark that indicated they were of the same family.

Griffin then addressed O'Riley. "Almost lost a soldier, did you?"

"Yes, sir. If it weren't for Corporal Marlow here and Big Elk, Private Bailey would be floating down to Utah as fish bait. Not much of a loss in my opinion. Sir, he's the worst bloody soldier in the company and manages to do the wrong thing at the wrong time. Can't ride worth a damn and always has trouble loading his carbine. If we were in a fight with the Indians, they'd have time for an afternoon nap before Bailey could chamber a round. Can't we transfer his ass to one of the infantry companies? He's an embarrassment to the US Cavalry and C Company."

"I'll see what I can do. Marlow, you're to be commended also. Sergeant tells me you're the best rider in the company."

"Thank you, sir. It's the horse."

Captain Griffin and Sergeant O'Riley rode off together, leaving Carroll with Marlow and Big Elk at the column's rear. Marlow noticed that Carroll said something to Big Elk in Ute. They both laughed as the Indian inspected his gold coin.

*   *   *

At the early morning formation the next day, Griffin announced that the troops would be crossing into the Utah Territory later in the afternoon. "Keep your eyes out for civilians . . . probably Mormons wanting to stir up the Ute with rumors. They've already fought two battles with the Utes, and they're not happy about more redskins coming into their territory."

The second night after crossing into Utah, it was Marlow's turn to pull guard duty—the eleven p.m. to seven a.m. shift. Guard duty was every soldier's least favorite, and Marlow was no exception. The combination of monotony and vigilance proved physically and mentally draining.

At about five thirty, Marlow heard a horse nicker off to his right and away from the remuda. When he rode toward the sound, he discovered in the quarter-moon light a rider on a pony pulling a travois and moving eastward, away from the Indian and Army camps. With his pistol drawn, Marlow rode up to the young Ute rider, and then signaled for him dismount and unfold the long canvas bag strapped to the travois. Inside the bag, a dead woman had been wrapped in a gray government-issue blanket, bound with rawhide straps, and adorned with short pieces of copper wire threaded through colorful beads.

Marlow searched the Indian for weapons and asked by way of sign language where the brave was headed with the travois. Marlow understood the answering Ute signal to be the Uncompahgre Valley. Marlow took his lariat from his saddle, put it over the pony's head, and led the Ute, mounted on his pony dragging the travois, to where Captain Griffin had set up company headquarters in the center of C Company's encampment.

"What in hell is going on, Corporal?" the captain asked with a scowl, clearly irritated by the early morning wake up.

"Sir, I found this Indian heading back in the direction of the reservation, dragging a travois loaded with the corpse of a woman, his mother, I think. Calls himself Running Bear. Did you give him permission to return to the Uncompahgre Valley?"

"No, I didn't, and I don't know who would have, except for the colonel. Tie his hands and take him to the colonel's headquarters. Kindred won't be happy. He ordered 'no prisoners,' remember, Corporal? You'd better be ready to do some explaining, exactly what you reported to me." After complimenting Marlow for his vigilance, the captain turned and entered his dark tent.

In the early dawn light, Marlow identified the colonel's headquarters by the regimental guidon flapping atop the large tent. He reported to the duty officer, Captain Olson, sitting outside, that he'd been ordered by Captain Griffin to bring this Ute rider and his travois to the colonel. Olson entered the tent and, within a minute, Kindred stepped outside as he slipped the suspenders of his riding britches over his shoulders.

"For Christ's sake, what is this all about?"

"Sir, this Indian may have been attempting to escape from our encampment this evening," Marlow said. "I discovered him about a half hour ago heading east on his pony, dragging a travois with the corpse of an elderly squaw, his mother, I believe. I was ordered by Captain Griffin to bring this situation to your attention, sir."

Carroll, half-dressed, immediately appeared from his tent adjacent to the colonel's. After questioning the Indian, he confirmed the identity of the corpse as the mother of Running Bear. The colonel ordered Marlow to cut the leather thongs on the prisoner's wrists but to keep him under guard with his carbine.

"You were trying to escape, were you?" The colonel pointed his finger at the Indian as he spoke. "You damned well know you've disobeyed my order."

The colonel's voice gained volume and an octave as he continued to berate the Indian. "You will not return to the reservation, but will be shot at daylight for attempting to escape from military authority."

He turned to Marlow. "Take him to Company C and tell Captain Griffin that this Indian is a temporary prisoner to be kept under close guard. In front of all the Ute and our regiment, this filthy Indian will be shot at daybreak." And then, turning to the interpreter, he said, "Mr. Carroll, make this known to this red nigger.

"And Marlow, I want to know why you didn't shoot this Indian on sight, as I had ordered for any Indian attempting to escape."

"Sir, since he was traveling with a travois, I thought it possible the Indian might have had written permission from you, and I thought it also possible he may have been given permission to leave our compound, but I couldn't confirm it. For that reason, and the fact that he was traveling with his dead mother, I thought it not right to shoot him on sight, sir."

"You 'thought,' did you? Soldier, let me remind you," Kindred shouted in Marlow's face, "I do the thinking for this regiment, not a corporal. You're damned lucky I'm not putting you up for a general court-martial for disobeying an order. What is your name?"

"Corporal Hiram Marlow, sir."

"You're Private Marlow as of right now. I expect you to obey all orders in the future, without thought and without question. Dismissed."

With his carbine by his side, Marlow saluted stoically, did an about-face, and stood inside the tent by the exit flap. Stunned by his sudden demotion, Marlow felt compelled to see if Kindred's temper might explode at Running Bear.

The colonel stood by his portable desk and glared at the Indian. Kindred's three finger stubs tapped the desktop like a judge wielding his gavel. And then, looking at the travois, he said, "As for this corpse, it will be disposed of immediately. I refuse to have the stinking corpse of a savage foul our Army compound. We will bury it or place it in a tree so that the vultures can feed on it, but it's not going to Utah or back to Colorado. Is that understood? Captain Olson, assemble a burial detail, and a four-man firing squad for seven o'clock tomorrow morning; and Mr. Carroll, make my statement very clear to the red son of a bitch."

"Yes, sir," Carroll replied, and then turned to the Indian with the colonel's message.

Carroll knew well enough not to give a word-for-word translation, for fear of making a bad situation worse. He hesitated for a moment while trying to think of a less inflammatory translation. During that pause, Running Bear, without warning, sprang like a mountain lion at the colonel, tackled him to the ground, and put a powerful chokehold on his throat. Soft gurgles emerged from the scarlet-faced colonel as the two men rolled on the ground.

Marlow dropped his carbine and yanked the Indian off Kindred, who, upon regaining his feet, staggered to the chair beside his cot. From the holster hanging on the chair, Kindred pulled out his service pistol with his left hand and ordered Marlow to retie the Indian's hands. "*Take him outside!*" Kindred shouted.

Kindred followed directly behind the Indian and Marlow. Once outside in the faint light, he ordered Marlow to push Running Bear to his knees and then to join Carroll and Olson back inside the tent.

Alone with the Ute, Kindred walked up to him, leaned over about six inches from Running Bear's face, and growled, "How dare you touch me, you dirty, filthy savage." Marlow, Carroll, and the duty officer looked out through the open tent flap as a crescendo of anger overtook Kindred. He spit on Running Bear and then slapped the Indian hard across the face with the back of his left hand. The Indian's head flinched from the blow. Immediately the colonel pulled his pistol from his holster, cocked the hammer, and leaned over, pointing the pistol's barrel at Running Bear's temple. The Indian's face contorted as he turned his head away from the pistol. Holding the weapon in both hands, Kindred pulled the trigger; the weapon flashed, and the Indian hit the ground. His brains slipped out through the exit wound into a pool of blood. Shocked by the scene, Olson, Marlow, and Carroll stepped out from the tent and faced a grinning colonel, the gun still in his left hand.

Kindred immediately ordered the duty officer to assemble a burial detail. "Have them buried together. I don't give a damn where. Just get them the hell out of here." Then the colonel barked at Carroll, "Bring Shavano to me immediately." With the killing of Running Bear, it did occur to Kindred that Shavano and his band might retaliate for the death. *Let them try it*, Kindred thought, *I'll have the perfect excuse to annihilate them.*

A soldier appeared and dragged Running Bear away, the path of blood highlighted by the rising sun. Another soldier carted away the travois and its corpse. Shavano appeared.

Kindred wasted no time with pleasantries. "Chief, did you know that the son-of-a-bitch Running Bear tried to escape our military authority early this morning and was captured and brought to me by the guard here, Private Marlow? In the presence of Mr. Carroll, Captain Olson, and Marlow, your sub-chief charged me, wrestled me to the ground, and tried to strangle me. In self-protection, I shot him. A burial detail has taken Running Bear's corpse and his dead mother to an unknown burial site."

Shavano stood mute and stunned as Carroll related the murder exactly as he witnessed it, not as Kindred described it. To make certain he understood everything the interpreter had said, the chief asked for clarification about the sequence of events, including Kindred's self-defense argument.

Shavano turned quickly to Kindred. Carroll translated. "Colonel, he, Running Bear, is my nephew and his mother is my sister. Yes, Running Bear want to go to Colorado with his mother. That is the Ute way. But you say we are under 'military authority' and must follow colonel's orders. We are recognized as independent tribe with support of Indian Bureau. They don't give us orders."

Kindred tried to interrupt, but Shavano continued to speak through Carroll. "In recent treaty and meetings, Colonel, we agreed to move peacefully, give up Uncompahgre Valley for new reservation in Utah. No one tell Ute we are under military authority. In spirit of goodwill and wish for peace, we give you our weapons, which you return to us when at new reservation. Now you capture my nephew and say he violate your orders." Shavano took a breath and spit out the words that Carroll reluctantly translated: "And then you murdered him with hands tied behind back."

The colonel listened to the translation from Carroll. Kindred's face turned red with rage and his upper body began to shake.

"Never in my entire career have I been so humiliated and threatened as I was this evening! Physically attacked—and by a red-skinned savage, at that. And now you, an Indian, think you have the authority to lecture *me* on my actions and responsibilities as a United States Army colonel."

Before continuing, Kindred waited as Carroll made his translation. "Chief, I was placed in charge of this move by General Sheridan himself. I have permission to use whatever methods I deem appropriate to transplant you and your filthy tribe to Utah. Your sub-chief, a relative of yours, I understand, tried to escape my authority. We captured him, and then he tried to kill me. In self-defense, I killed him. Do I make myself understood to you? In *self-defense*. Make that clear to him, Mr. Carroll. Also let me make it very clear that if there are any future attempts to escape my authority or bring injury to my soldiers, I will not hesitate to kill the guilty and cut in half the rations of your entire band. Understand?" Carroll translated.

Shavano gave no indication he heard a word of it. Without a glance at Kindred or the other soldiers, he reached for the rawhide necklace around his neck on which hung the Peace Medal presented to him by President Grant, ripped it from his body, threw it to the ground, and then shouted in English, "We demand justice, Colonel!"

As Shavano stalked out of the tent, he spit on the Peace Medal, mounted his pony, and rode off to his headquarters within the Indian encampment. Kindred shouted at Shavano, who, without turning in his saddle, spit once again. Carroll's eyes followed his tribesman with a mixture of pride and fear, while Kindred stomped off to his tent.

It did not take long before word had spread through the regiment that an Indian sub-chief had been captured and shot by the colonel in self-defense. When soldiers learned from Carroll the victim had had his hands tied behind his back, they questioned how Kindred could claim self-defense. It was one thing to chase after Indians trying to escape in violation of a military order, who refused to stop after warning shots. But most soldiers recognized it was a different matter when an Indian put up no resistance, surrendered peacefully, and then was insulted and murdered in cold blood.

One soldier muttered, "We need to kill all dem redskins any way we can."

Marlow overheard the comment but could only shake his head.

After dark, Griffin rode the perimeter of his company and informed O'Riley to be on the lookout for Indians trying to escape back to the reservation. In the early morning hours, two Infantry squad tents mysteriously caught fire, causing a scare among the troops but no injuries. Kindred thought about how the Indians might retaliate for Running Bear's death, but he also recognized how little trouble the unarmed Indians could cause.

The colonel didn't know that Carroll had conversed with Shavano and advised him not to retaliate against Kindred and his well-armed troops. "Kindred wants you to retaliate," Carroll told Shavano. "That way he'll have an excuse to attack and kill you all. Remember the Army is always looking for an excuse to fight Indians."

Shortly after dawn the next day, the Indians had packed their horses and dogs, killed their fires, and signaled to Kindred they were ready. The column experienced no trouble as it moved down Douglas Creek to the junction with the White River, where they made camp. That night, two more squad tents burned as Indians danced and beat drums around their campfires.

When Kindred learned of the fires, he said to his senior staff, "I have half a mind to burn *their* camps and kill the lot of them. But then again, it could be those god-damned Mormons." Since no one was injured, Kindred's deputy commander advised the colonel to take no retaliatory action. Still, Kindred shorted the Ute rations just to remind them the Army controlled their destiny. And he called in Shavano for a lecture about the fires and threatened action against any Indian seen near a soldier's tent. But throughout the next three days on the march, Kindred found no excuse to let loose the regiment's firepower against the Ute. He pushed on at a faster pace, tiring both the Ute and his troopers.

By midafternoon of the ninth day of the march, the column reached the new reservation site.

Marlow was struck by the uninviting landscape—flat, arid, devoid of vegetation except for isolated clumps of wilted sage and salt grass. No birds, not even a mosquito. The company commander commented that the enemies of the Ute, probably the Mormons but possibly another Indian tribe, had, like the Romans, covered the landscape with alkali to make it sterile.

Marlow commented to Carroll, "I can't believe the Ute agreed to this desolate site."

"We didn't," Carroll responded. "We have no choice. Indian Commission in Washington selected site. Shavano tell us the new reservation to be rich in grass and wildlife. That is what two Indian commissioners, Mr. Mannypenny and Otto Mears, tell him. They say to Shavano, 'The Utah lands are better than what you leave behind in Colorado. Utah reservations have many big grass valleys and much wildlife in surrounding mountains.' But Mears lied to Shavano. The original 1879 Peace Treaty, which Ute agreed to, say our new home to be in 'Grand Valley at junction of Colorado and Gunnison rivers in Colorado.' We passed through there many days ago. As you did see, it is very beautiful and lush. But we leave it behind us."

Carroll cast his eye over the barren landscape and watched a couple of braves dig into the soil to inspect it. One grabbed a handful of the alkali dirt and handed it to an elderly Ute, who shook his head and threw his hands to the sky.

Carroll continued. "Right after we signed treaty, however, Mears visited Grand Valley and recognized its good soil. Mears see it as future settlement area for white farmers, who he want as new customers for his trading company. Mears reported to Senate committee that Grand Valley is 'not suitable' for Indians. He had Senate amend the original treaty to read 'Grand Valley or its vicinity.' In the midst of treaty changes, Ouray died. No one defended interests of Ute when government interpreted words 'or its vicinity' to include Utah Territory. And that is where we are right now . . . in the 'vicinity.'"

So at this site, Marlow thought, *they're a long way from any white settlements. They'll be safe here, but even with government rations, can they survive in this dry country?*

In an exchange with Carroll and Baxter, Shavano was quick to express his opinion of the new site. Through Carroll, he communicated, "This land is not what you described to us back at Los Piños. It is dry, vacant salt flat. No trees. No grass. What our horses eat? And where is wildlife you say be everywhere? Where is water to irrigate like we have in Colorado? Evil spirits must live here.

"Only one good thing here. We are now far away from whites and your diseases. There be a new one every generation."

When Shavano's sub-chiefs approached to report that about a third of the Ute horse herd had turned up missing after the march from Colorado to Utah, Shavano demonstrated his quick temper, shouting at two sub-chiefs and waving them off.

Baxter attempted to calm him by declaring, "What you see here is only a small portion of the hundred-thousand-acre reservation. We stop here only to show you a portion of your new allotment. I can assure you that even here, with an irrigation system, this land will flourish and so shall your livestock. Those mountains to the north are home to elk, deer, and bear. The river waters, not far from here, are filled with fish and beaver." Baxter added that with the construction of irrigation canals and ditches, an abundance of grass and winter hay could be produced.

Shavano clearly was not convinced as he rode off to complain to the colonel at his temporary headquarters.

Meanwhile, the company officers directed the unloading of the wagons: lumber, still wet from the river crossing, for a new agent's office and quarters; Indian rations for issuance the next day; a John Deere plow; soggy bags of seed; warped office furniture; a heavy steel safe; and two locked trunks with weapons and ammunition.

In his command tent, Kindred lay out on his camp table a drawing of the projected agency compound for Shavano to inspect. It included the future addition of a guardhouse and infirmary, the latter facility, he said to Shavano through Carroll, "a real luxury for an Indian agency."

"Rations will be issued tomorrow morning at eight. As you know, there will be no fresh meat since the eight steers we trailed coming here were slaughtered, against my orders, and eaten by your band."

Shavano snapped back angrily. Carroll translated, "No, your soldiers. From Indian camp, I smelled beef cooking in your camp. My people are hungry; soldiers the ones with greasy fingers and full bellies."

Kindred disregarded the comment and pulled out a map.

"The weapons and ammunition we took from you and your band before leaving the Uncompahgre Valley you will find hidden right here." Kindred pointed to a spot on a hand-drawn map. "The site is about a day's ride back toward Colorado. You will not go to retrieve these weapons until the day after we, the Army, have departed. If there is any attempt to return to the Uncompahgre Valley after our departure, your tribal members will be shot on sight. Understand?"

Shavano didn't respond to the threat, but not knowing how to read a white man's map, he had questions about the location of the weapons.

"You can't mistake the site," Kindred said. "In a small cave fifteen feet above the river at the point where it turns sharply north. You'll be able to confirm the spot by a tall sandstone pinnacle. You'll also see our wagon tracks to the site. Any more questions?"

Shavano fixed the cave within the framework of his mental geography. He stood silent, nodded, and walked away, refusing the hand of Kindred.

Kindred, left alone with Carroll, tried to understand Shavano and his Indian ways. "He has a quick temper. That is evident," Kindred observed and then turned to Carroll. "Can Shavano continue to control his people?"

Not even Carroll could advise. He offered to Kindred only: "Ute know when to fight and when to stay peaceful."

FOUR

With the freight wagons empty, no Indians to guard, good weather, and a smaller remuda to trail, the column moved at a faster pace back to the cantonment. The troops looked forward to collecting their pay and mail, and maybe having a few days off for a visit to the brothels and bars of Ouray. To break the monotony of the march, officers allowed troopers to capture the stray Indian ponies that had fallen behind on the march into Utah.

Following the same route they'd taken into Utah, the regiment rode through the steep sandstone valleys and alkali flats along the borderland of Colorado-Utah, where for centuries wind- and snowstorms had sculpted the red rock into sandstone monuments, some of which resembled animals sacred to the Ute. As the troopers rode into the morning sun, Marlow wished he could capture the heat and carry it back to the cantonment for what would be his last two months in the Army, and certain to be cold ones.

Marlow took the opportunity to ride his other horse, a green-broke three-year-old gelding, which Sergeant O'Riley had assigned to him at the cantonment. His bunk-mate, Mike Dolan, rode alongside Marlow so that his horse might help calm Marlow's young mount. Dolan also looked for some pointers on training his own young colt. As they rode together, they talked of their plans after their enlistment expired.

Dolan said that after his discharge from the Army, he'd head to the gold and silver mines in the nearby San Juans. "I hear from the miners in Ouray there's good money to be made if you're not too fussy about your accommodations. Can't be no worse than this shit hole, right? What you goin' to do, Hiram?"

"Figure I'll probably go back home to Iowa and my family's farm. My parents are getting on in age, and I know they're looking forward to my return. My brother is there to help out, but they're still shorthanded, especially at planting and harvest time. I sure would like to stay in Colorado to make some money in the mines. Nice country here. It sure beats the hellish heat of Iowa. But then again, the Colorado winters are something else.

"You ever been in the mines?" Marlow asked Dolan.

"No, but it can't be all that more miserable than Army life. I know how to handle a pick and shovel. In the last two years, I've shoveled enough fucking dirt and rock for this damned outfit to tunnel through the Rockies all the way east to Fort Garland. I got a cousin over near Denver in the mines. I figure if that scrawny son of a bitch can make good money and survive, I sure as hell can also. You don't need to be no engineer. Just pack a little muscle and ambition."

Then Dolan turned in his saddle and faced Marlow. "What do you think of Kindred's shooting that sub-chief?"

"If you or I did what Kindred did, we'd be brought before a military court, found guilty of murder, and placed before a firing squad before sundown. Sure, we killed those two Indians trying to escape at the river the other day, but Running Bear, who voluntarily and without resistance surrendered to me, that's a different matter."

Dolan agreed. "You can bet a month's pay Kindred won't be punished. Maybe a slap on his two-fingered hand, but that's about it. You and I know that the Army doesn't court-martial its own senior officers, never has as far as I know, and never will. They'll court-martial a poor Army teamster for abusing a mule before they'll lay a hand on Kindred. Army officers don't give a shit about justice, only promotion to a higher rank."

In the middle of the next day, Carroll rode up to Marlow as the column made their way across some sagebrush flats. "Last evening I helped Chief Shavano with letter to President Hayes, and copy to General Sherman. He write about murder of nephew, Running Bear, by Colonel Kindred. Shavano want Colonel to be punished and put on trial. He say Washington long ago promised Ute with protection of white man's law. Now he want that protection. He ask the president what is to stop another Army officer from picking me out for a minor violation of your many rules and regulations, put gun to my head, and pull trigger? Shavano also say that if a Ute murdered the colonel, we know the outcome. The Ute demand same punishment for Kindred.

"Then Shavano at letter end say, 'If no justice for Ute, I promise trouble in Colorado. Other nearby tribes learn about murder and cause big trouble with your Army.' Shavano named you, me, and Captain Olson as witnesses to murder."

Carroll continued with his own thoughts. "If Sherman and the president feel real mad like us, maybe Sherman order court-martial, I hope."

"That's unlikely," Marlow responded. "The Army is not going to court-martial its most famous Indian killer. After all, that's the mission of the Army: kill Indians!"

"Yes, but White Father not at war with Ute."

"Maybe it's not a declared war, but we all know the Army likes to kill Indians when they have the opportunity. Thank you for telling me about the letter. But don't get your hopes up. Nothing will come of it, certainly not a court-martial. I'll be leaving the Army in forty-two days when my enlistment is up, and I'll be glad to be done with everything about this. How about you?"

"After I collect rations and pay at agency, I to quit as interpreter. Not to take any more crap from military men like Kindred or translate lies to Ute. I no more want to be around the bastard. After first of the year, I head to my former home near the old Los Piños Agency, forty-five miles northeast of the current agency, and try and make life as hunter, like father. Still good game there. I hear there is big demand back East and Europe for beaver pelts. Also elk and deer hides, if well tanned, mean big money. White hunters may give us trouble for coming back to old reservation land, but I try to avoid trouble."

Marlow understood Carroll's fear but he could also understand the whites' attraction, including his own, to the lush, vacated reservation land.

★   ★   ★

At the corrals, the soldiers removed their saddles, made a mental note of what gear needed repair, checked their horses' feet for loose or missing shoes, and then brushed down their mounts before placing feed bags with oats over their muzzles. The soldiers moved slowly toward the company formation where, amid a snow shower, the company sergeant announced meal hours and pay call.

"Saturday morning will be given over to maintenance and repair duties," O'Riley shouted. "A leave schedule starting Saturday afternoon will be posted outside the adjutant's office. And I want your fugghan arses back here by midnight, not a minute later. Bailey, you keep that little pecker of yours buttoned up and stay away from those bars. You'll get all them girls excited. Dismissed."

The troops broke ranks and lugged weapons and other gear to their quarters.

Marlow picked up his mail at company headquarters, a squad tent that looked as if it had been present in every battle of the Civil War. He recognized his mother's handwriting.

Sept.5, 1880
My Dear Hiram,

We have had no word from you since early August when you said you were being transferred to Colorado. I hope the Indian duty there is safer than your encounters with the Comanche in New Mexico and Texas. Here at home they do have a terrible reputation for savagery.

Just one more week and the harvest will be over. We've been slowed down by Sam injuring a leg tendon, but he's now back to normal and pulling his weight. Father is very happy with our record crop and the high prices for corn and hogs. He thinks we may be able to pay off the entire bank loan when our payment comes due the end of the year. Also, since Father is slowing down, he'd like to see if he can hire Bobby back for spring planting. Bobby works in town now at the elevator and asks about you all the time.

We have worked so hard since we first settled here on the original homestead. Doubling the size of the farm thanks to your Father's service in the war, and then planting more acreage and buying some hogs has finally paid off. Unlike the poor folks in the southern part of the state who've suffered the drought, we can thank God for the wonderful moisture we had this spring and summer. Our prayers were answered. Thankfully we are in good health except for Father's arthritis.

I pray also for your safety and health and look forward to your return after the first of the year. I trust you'll get yourself to Denver and then a train home to Newton.

Your brother continues to grow and eat everything in sight. The Army would reject him for his appetite. As always, he is a wonderful help to Father, especially with the horses. Just like you.

I need to mention that Father recently had a visit from Joel Swinger, our neighbor to the north and west. He wants to buy our farm (with animals) and has offered Father a very generous price. Father says he will not make a decision until you return in January. Be prepared to discuss this with Father, your brother, and me.

Please keep us informed of your activities. Neighbors ask about you frequently, especially your former English teacher, Miss Haley, and the Reverend Nelson.

We so miss you and pray for your safety.

With love,
Mother

The letter reminded Marlow how much he missed his family. Sooner rather than later he needed to return to Iowa.

FIVE

For Marlow, the last days of his enlistment passed slowly as the boredom of garrison duty weighed heavily on his time. Most troopers in the company expected to be transferred to the military encampment being constructed within the Ute's new reservation in Utah. Captain Griffin encouraged Marlow to reenlist for another three years, with the promise of a thirty-dollar bonus and a promotion to his former rank of corporal. However, Marlow's recurring nightmare of the Comanche in Texas cancelled out any thoughts he might have about gaining some extra money in return for guarding Indians or, more likely, fighting them. He figured, based on local Ouray newspapers and the accounts from Dolan, that he could make that bonus money and probably another two hundred dollars by working in the Ouray mines for nine months or less. With money in his pocket, he'd head home to Iowa, look after his parents, make his living on the family farm, or maybe buy a place of his own.

Sawing and chopping firewood through December built up his upper-body strength in preparation for work in the mines. On the evening before his release, Marlow's squad mates hosted a party for him inside the tent that served as a mess hall. The liquor flowed freely, and both Sergeant O'Riley and Captain Griffin lifted their glasses to toast Marlow's service and wished him good luck in the future. At the morning formation on Marlow's last day, O'Riley paid his highest compliment to the company's best rider. "Marlow, you're a damned fine trooper," he said as he patted him on the shoulder.

Army policy allowed a departing soldier to purchase at a discount a horse, saddle, and bridle with which to make his way home. Marlow needed only a horse and selected the stoutest of the three-year-old geldings he had trained; he also purchased from the quartermaster extra socks and underwear. He was allowed to keep his uniforms and, to Marlow's surprise, his buffalo-skin great coat. The night before his discharge, Marlow had bid farewell to each of his squad mates and collected the addresses of some of his buddies, including Carroll.

"Carroll, I may go to the mines in Ouray and I wonder if you'll be in these parts after you leave the Army?"

"You can find me near old Los Piños Agency before it move to Uncompahgre Valley. It is place of my old home. Livestock thrive on the grass. Good hunting also."

"I might like to get there sometime to see you."

"You best wait 'til spring. Snow will be to the stirrups right now. You need camel, and there are none around here that I see. I understand Army have camels in Arizona.

Personally, I take a long-legged English horse rather than double-humped sand buggy."

"Hope to see you in the spring or summer." Marlow laughed as he put his hand on Carroll's shoulder. The half-breed returned the friendly gesture.

Marlow had been debating with himself for months whether to work in the mines or go straight back to Iowa. As much as he couldn't stand working under the thumb of his father, neither could he, as a son, forego his responsibilities to his parents, especially after Bobby quit to work at the grain elevator. Marlow promised his family he'd have some savings after his enlistment that could go toward helping with the farm mortgage. Somehow, however, the savings never materialized. His mother had suggested that high grain prices this fall might allow the family to pay off the entire debt. Still, Marlow thought, he could use extra money from working in the mines to buy some land, or maybe homestead on his own. Whether he homesteaded or remained on the family farm, the new machines coming on the market, which promised to increase production, were considered a good investment for the future but damned expensive. He sat down and wrote his parents.

Dear Mother and Father,

Over a month ago, I returned from a long march into the Utah Territory, west of here. We had to move some Indians who were no longer welcome in the new State of Colorado. The Indians didn't want to leave their historic homeland, but the President said they had to move. So the Army got the nasty job of moving these unhappy people. They marched without much fuss to some land in Utah, not half as fertile as what they left behind.

Today I finished my Army enlistment in good health and with a few dollars in my pocket. I had hoped to have more savings at the end of my second enlistment but personal expenses (clothing, extra food, horse gear) absorbed almost all savings from my monthly pay. But I do want to have some money in my pocket when I return home.

I've decided, therefore, to work in the local gold and silver mines near Ouray, about twenty miles south of our post in the San Juan Mountains. With any luck, I should be able to save well over two hundred dollars between now and next summer. I'm in excellent physical condition after my Army service and should have no trouble finding a position with one of the more profitable mining companies.

I know you'll be disappointed with my decision, but it is only another six or seven months before I'm home. I hope Father can wait that long before making a decision about selling the farm.

The country around here is beautiful. In the autumn, the leaves on the cottonwood trees are all a bright yellow, and the brilliant-red leaves on the oak brush make it appear they're on fire. But now, all the trees are bare and with snow in the mountains, and it won't be long before we are trapped by snow. The weather is cool during the days and hard frosts at night. I'm in good health despite the Army food. Father wouldn't feed his hogs what the Army throws out to us for meals.

You can write me c/o the Town of Ouray Post Office, Ouray, Colorado.

I love you all and will miss you over Christmas. Please write!

Your devoted son,
Hiram

After his release from the Army in early December, Marlow read an advertisement in the Ouray newspaper for jobs at the Columbine Mine.

Highest paid mining jobs in the San Juans. Quality food with comfortable accommodations. Contact Mr. Isman at the Beaumont Hotel for more information and an interview.

The town of Ouray named itself in honor of the Ute chief. By playing to his vanity, the town fathers hoped that Chief Ouray and his band of Ute down valley would remain peaceful. A friendly relationship with the tribe would allow the town to prosper from its silver and gold mines and continue to supply the monthly rations to the Indians. After the US government "bought" back the San Juan mining district in 1873 from the Ute, helped along with a lifelong "salary" to Chief Ouray, the town and the Indians maintained a peaceful coexistence.

The town thrived off its mineral wealth, particularly gold. By the 1880s, brick came to replace clapboard and canvas as downtown Ouray transformed itself from a collection of tents and shacks, randomly arranged as if by a hurricane, to a certified town. It prided itself on the splendor of some of its private residences and the size and elegance of the new Beaumont Hotel, headquarters for visiting absentee mine owners and stockholders. Also the snow-covered mountain peaks surrounding Ouray came to attract their first tourists from Denver, an income source that partially replaced the loss of sales to the Indian agency.

In his lavishly appointed hotel room, heated by the hot water springs beneath the town, Mr. Isman, an ex-miner, asked Marlow if he'd had any mining experience.

"None, sir."

"What makes you think you're fit for the mines?"

"Sir, I've just come out of the Army. I'm in good physical shape and accustomed to hard work. I have a recommendation from my former company commander." Marlow handed Mr. Isman a small envelope.

"We can use a stout lad like you. You'll be paid two fifty a day or sixty dollars a month, including room and board. You're to be outside this hotel tomorrow morning at nine thirty. You'll ride up to the mine with the supply train. There'll be some extra mules. Grab one for a ride. All you need to do is follow the pack train up into the mountains. At the mine, the supervisor will inform you as to your starting job and where to bunk. Good luck, Marlow."

What to do with my horse? Marlow asked himself. He had no use for Chunk at the mine, but neither did he want to sell him after all the effort he'd put into training the gelding. Instead he boarded the horse with a stable in Ouray. By the time he'd paid the required advance to the stable and purchased work boots, an extra work shirt, and canvas pants, Marlow had spent almost his entire Army savings.

Winter had arrived a month early at the Columbine Mine, which was located due south of Ouray in the mountains at 10,800 feet. A sturdy wooden shed protected the entrance from snow and wind, which had produced deep drifts on the backside of structures. Miners and burros stood in the cold around the mine entrance, awaiting their shift. The winds would sing to Marlow at home in Iowa, but in the Colorado mountains, they only growled, spitting ice and snow in his face from all directions.

Marlow deposited his Army haversack containing his few possessions under his assigned bunk in the dormitory. The late-afternoon frost reminded Marlow that his Army buffalo-skin coat would be needed as an extra blanket.

The mine supervisor entered the dormitory, a flimsy wooden shack with canvas doors, and gave Marlow a short, but close, visual inspection. He asked Marlow about his experience in the mines.

"None, sir. Fresh out of the Army."

"So that's why they sent you up here from Ouray. Honorably discharged were you?"

"Yes, sir. Came with a good recommendation from my company commander." Marlow reached into his pocket for his discharge papers and the short note from Captain Griffin.

"I can see you're a strong, healthy lad, not one of those frail, skin-and-bones types who come out here from the East in their city rags. Farm boy, are you?"

"Originally from Iowa, sir, where I grew up on our family farm. Good country, it is. A bit warmer than this place."

"Son, anywhere else is warmer than this godforsaken rock pile. But there is money to be made here if you're willing to work and be on time for your shift. I'm going to place you with the B Team. You'll work as a mucker, shoveling ore into ore cars, which trammers—other miners on your shift—will push to the main shaft. In some cases burros will substitute for a trammer. Your foreman, everyone calls him Big Jim, will show you everything you need to know tomorrow on your seven a.m. shift. You'll have Sunday off. Breakfast is at six, and supper at seven.

Both meals are in the mess tent. You'll take lunch with you into the mine.

"Follow Big Jim's instructions. He's good mentor. The last mucker with the B Team got himself badly injured three days ago when he didn't listen to instructions. And one other thing: if I see you talking to one of them union organizers who sneak up here from time to time, I'll kick your ass back down the mountain. Any questions?"

"Yes, sir. Is mail delivered to the mine?"

"Yes. Twice a week. Have it addressed to Columbine Mine, Ouray, Colorado. Anything else, Marlow?"

"No, sir."

"Good luck to you and, remember, listen to Big Jim." The supervisor walked away and returned to the mine's storehouse, where he made his office.

Marlow entered the mess hall, a long, wooden structure with a dirty canvas hanging from the roof on the west side covering a partially missing wall. He learned from another miner that the canvas marked where the avalanche had hit last week, killing two miners. Half of the wall had been replaced, and the other half was still under construction. Marlow sat at one of the plank tables and introduced himself to those around him: a husky Negro from Texas, two German-speaking brothers from the Austrian mining area bordering Italy, a young fuzzy-faced kid from Brooklyn, a former seaman from Nantucket Island in Massachusetts, and a Kentucky corn cracker. Big Jim made himself known with a squeeze from his hand, which was the size of a pie tin and the force of which could, no doubt, strangle a buffalo. A thick, dirty, tobacco-stained beard blackened most of his face, and a frayed canvas jacket covered his broad shoulders.

"Are you the new man Mr. Isman sent up from Ouray?"

"Yes, sir, that's me. Hiram Marlow," he responded, looking up at Big Jim's six-foot frame.

"You'll want to get your ass over to the company store after dinner and buy your supplies. See you in the morning at the main entrance to the tunnel."

"Yes, sir."

Marlow found the company store and the high prices that went with it. He purchased a pair of gloves, a lunch bucket, and a felt hat. He'd brought his own water canteen and work jacket from the Army. Two pieces of chocolate completed his purchases. The total cost, he was informed, would be subtracted from his wages.

After a supper of canned beef, potatoes, and a grayish vegetable he could not identify, Marlow, exhausted from his first two days of civilian life, returned to the bunkhouse. An Irish bunkmate pointed to some straw inside the door and suggested to Marlow, "Take some of them there prairie feathers and make your bedding. But I'd inspect it first, mate. They may be loaded with ticks and lice. I don't know where them damned critters come from. Can't seem to get rid of the little buggers. One hell of a sex life they have."

Marlow picked up an armload of straw, took it outside, and gave it a thorough inspection, discarding one handful and taking the remainder to his wooden bunk. Within minutes he'd fallen asleep in his clothes, covered by his buffalo-skin overcoat. He awoke suddenly to his recurring nightmare about the Comanche scalping party. He undressed, checked again for lice, and slid beneath the dark-brown buffalo hide.

Breakfast consisted of a tan-colored mush that Marlow mistook for a cereal but which others identified as ground-up potato skins with a hint of brown sugar. He learned that a covering of milk improved the taste not only of the potato skins but of other breakfast and supper treats offered up by the Columbine gang of incompetent cooks. Marlow figured they had made their way into the San Juan's mining district via the Army.

At the mine entrance, Marlow met up with Big Jim.

"Here are three candles for you, a pick, a shovel, a whistle, and a sledge. Don't lose 'em. Follow me."

They entered into the belly of the mountain in an ore bucket that moved up and down inside the mine by way of a cable and a series of bells. At the bottom of the two-hundred-foot shaft, the two men walked down the middle of a set of rail tracks. At a junction about forty yards into the cold, damp tunnel, they took a right turn into another narrower tunnel. Big Jim helped Marlow adjust and better secure his candle to his felt hat. After stumbling along in the poor light for another ten minutes, they came upon metal ore carts sitting empty on the rails.

"Here's your home, me lad. Your job is to collect up all the rock ore you see around you and load up the cart. When it is filled, give this whistle a single long blow. A trammer will appear to remove the cart. Then you start filling the next cart. You'll find some of the ore blocks are too big to get into the cart. You'll pick and sledge them into smaller sizes and then load them. Don't worry about the explosions you'll hear from time to time at the head of the tunnel. That's the blasting crew producing some more ore for you to load. I expect, given your stout body, you'll load about two carts an hour. If you get injured in any way, blow your whistle three times. There's a medical attendant in the mine for every shift. Now time's a wasting; let's get on with it."

"Where do I relieve myself?" Marlow asked.

"Off to the side of the rail tracks," Big Jim casually responded.

Marlow had never experienced working in a dark hole. The candle provided more shadows than illumination, which only increased Marlow's anxiety amid the dank workplace. He didn't know if he'd ever get accustomed to the smell of human and animal feces, burnt powder, and water-soaked timber. Within ten minutes he could feel cold water inside his boots.

By the end of his twelve-hour shift, his hands had blistered and his lower back stiffened. Bent over, he shuffled to the lift, careful to pull off his gloves, which had adhered to the bloody scabs on the broken blisters inside. At the bunkhouse, he washed his hands with soap as best he could in the freezing water and wrapped them in cloth strips, fashioned from his only towel. He changed into a pair of dry socks and his old Army riding boots. Dinner satisfied his appetite but not his curiosity as to the identity of the meat. A tablemate suggested, "It's probably one of them dead burros we hauled up the shaft earlier this afternoon."

By the fifth day, with his hands wrapped and his gloves and boots made more pliable and water resistant with some axle grease, Marlow paced himself into a smooth routine of filling two carts every hour. No one seemed to complain about his pace. In fact, Big Jim complimented him on the steadiness of his work.

By Saturday, Marlow looked forward to an evening of entertainment in Ouray. The Columbine ran two wagons into town after supper with return runs to the mine scheduled for midnight and two a.m. Most miners spent Saturday night in Ouray and, after sobering up, caught one of the two Sunday-morning wagons back to the mine.

The saloon of choice in Ouray took its name from the color of the beer it served. Those who patronized the Bucket of Blood soaked up gallons of the local brew, supplemented with tomato juice for its color not its taste, while a piano player pounded out German and Irish favorites. At the bar Marlow encountered Mike Dolan, his former bunkmate back at the cantonment and the one who had informed Marlow about the opportunities available in the Ouray mines.

"Dolan, good to see you again. I see by your jacket you're in the mines."

"Couldn't resist some additional suffering. I'm working up at the Yankee Girl Mine. The pay's OK. The food, I think, they buy from the Army. It's about what I expected, but I'm making good money. Plan to quit next summer and then return home. So what are you doing here? Thought you were headed home to Iowa after your discharge. I can tell by your jacket you're sure as hell not a store clerk or a dentist. Miner too, right?"

"Yeah, up at the Columbine mucking. Pay's good but that's about all. Buy you a drink?"

"Thanks."

A middle-aged woman came up to both men, batting her eyes a couple of times to bring attention to her long false black lashes. She appeared not to have noticed that her ample breasts had partially escaped from beneath a tight sequined blouse. She eased up to the two men, maneuvering her right breast against Marlow's shoulder. He thought her halfway attractive and started up a conversation.

"Where you from?"

"Right here in Ouray," she responded.

"No. I mean, before you came here."

"Brooklyn."

"New York?"

"You're one smart kid."

"What brought you out to this desolate place?"

"Follow the money, like everyone else," she said with some enthusiasm and then added, "There's plenty here with these miners, more than with the sailors back East." Before Marlow could respond, she asked, "Which one of youse handsome guys is goin' to buy me a whiskey?" Marlow ordered another round from the bartender, who knew the routine.

After taking a gulp from the double-shot whiskey glass and looking directly at Dolan, she offered, "I got me a nice soft, clean bed." Then she reached down and put her hand on Dolan's crotch. "You want a great back rub, I give it. You want a nice warm, wet hole for that hard pecker, I got that too. What say?"

A long silence followed the offer.

"How much?" Dolan asked, more out of curiosity than desire.

"Ten bucks, plus two fifty."

"Why the two fifty?"

"The town's lookin' for some additional revenue. Started taxin' us girls the first of the year."

"Ten bucks. Are you kidding? Has inflation hit Colorado? Your services cost half that in New Mexico," he responded.

"That may be true in New Mexico, kid, but I ain't no filthy Mexican or Indian."

"You're a bit pricey for me, sister."

"Me too," Marlow added.

Clearly not pleased with the outcome of her sales pitch, the soiled dove gathered up her drink and sashayed down the bar to another potential customer.

They stayed at the Bucket until after midnight, brushing off other solicitations, discussing their mining jobs, and reminiscing about their time together in the Army. Marlow asked if Dolan had heard any news about their cavalry company, about O'Riley, and what dumb-ass orders Kindred had issued to make life for the soldiers more intolerable.

"He's no longer at the cantonment. Kindred left suddenly just after your discharge. Usually when a post commander leaves there's a parade and a bunch of fancy ceremonies. Not with Kindred. He just up and disappeared. Rumor had it around camp that he was under some kind of investigation for the killing of that Indian."

"I hope the son of a bitch gets brought before a court-martial board," Marlow responded.

"Not likely. The investigation probably means a general's star for the bastard," Dolan countered.

Before catching the wagon back to the mine, Marlow checked in at the livery stable. His horse appeared a bit gaunt, a condition Marlow mentioned to the proprietor.

"He's a hard keeper that one of yours. I feed him like every other critter here, but I can't keep weight on him. I'll worm him and put him on some extra feed if you want, but it'll cost more."

Marlow added the extra cost for the worming medicine and feed to the advance for January.

The freezing wagon ride back to the mine sobered him, but the unwelcome hangover that greeted him Sunday morning lingered throughout the day. The next day at the end of his shift, he climbed on the ore bucket with another miner. Two bells sounded. As they lifted to twenty feet off the shaft's bottom, the cable attached to the bucket snapped. The lift shot to the bottom. The impact threw the two miners out of the steel conveyance. Marlow hit the wall and then bounced back against the side of the bucket. As he lay unconscious, the other injured shift mate, Pete Rocco, poured some cold water on Marlow's skinned forehead. When he regained consciousness, Marlow could feel the pain of a fracture in his left leg and a broken collarbone.

Atop the shaft, the sound of three blows of a whistle and the sight of the broken cable signaled the accident. The lift attendant at the top dropped down a new cable, and within a minute a miner had it attached to the slightly damaged bucket. It took them ten minutes to carefully load Marlow, the most seriously injured, and Rocco. Two whistle signals sounded, and the bucket rose slowly to the top. Rocco, with only minor injuries, tried to comfort Marlow, but without success. The pain only increased for Marlow as the lift jolted and bounced off the shaft's side walls on its slow upward journey toward fresh air.

At the top, Big Jim helped unload Marlow and Rocco. He took them to the Columbine infirmary—a log shack with a fireplace and three cots, two of which were occupied by patients suffering from dysentery. A male nurse cut off Marlow's canvas pants, inspected the break, and began to fashion a temporary splint composed of two boards wrapped by cloth strips. After the nurse splinted Marlow's leg and put some iodine on his scalp cuts, he announced, "Not much more I can do for you. We need to get you to the doctor in Ouray as soon as possible."

Marlow asked, "What about my shoulder?"

"No one told me about your shoulder." The nurse removed Marlow's dirty work shirt and felt the broken collarbone. "The doc in Ouray can fix that up too. Not too bad a break, mate. You'll be back mucking in no time at all. Anything else?"

"Thanks. But I'm freezing. Can someone fetch my buffalo-skin coat in the dorm?" *How nice*, he thought, *to be lying on a horsehair mattress and in a place where the walls don't drip and there's no smell of burro shit.* He briefly dozed off with his arms crossed on his chest.

SIX

The wagon carrying the two injured miners made its way slowly down the rocky and rutted road to Ouray. The hour-long trip left Marlow's broken leg numbed with cold, while his shoulder throbbed with heat. Rocco sat motionless as he swore in his native Italian about losing wages because of the accident. The wagon pulled up to a small frame house. "Hospital" read the wooden sign above the door. Marlow sat up in his makeshift stretcher and said he preferred to hobble into the hospital rather than take the chance of being mishandled by the wagon driver or his teenage assistant. A short, heavyset, smiling woman, dressed in a nun's habit, greeted both miners at the entrance, identified herself as Sister Katherine, and accompanied Marlow to an empty bed in the ward.

"You rest, my boy, and we'll have Doc Hill here within the hour. I bet you could use a cup of hot tea and a biscuit?"

"Yes, ma'am. Where am I?"

"You're in the Miner's Hospital run by the Sisters of Mercy."

Without being told, Marlow realized his job at the mine had disappeared with his injuries. He figured the Columbine owed him six days' salary of fifteen dollars, less his charges at the company store of almost eight dollars. He planned to scratch off a note to Big Jim requesting the balance due him.

The doctor, his gray beard covering half his chest, looked to be in his late sixties and was dressed in a frayed black wool suit. Without introducing himself, he immediately pressed a stethoscope to Marlow's chest.

"Doc, it's the leg, not the chest that's broken."

"Son, please, let me do my job without interruption. Good strong heartbeat. And no temperature, I assume," the doctor announced after he removed the cold stethoscope from Marlow's chest and then ran his hand over Marlow's forehead. "How you feelin'?"

"Feel OK, 'cept for the cold ride down the mountain and the throbbing in my shoulder."

The doctor looked at the broken collarbone and said, "You'll have to keep your arm in a sling until the bone heals. Probably two to three weeks. Now, for the leg, let me take a look." He pulled back the covers, removed the temporary splint, and inspected Marlow's dirty swollen leg.

"Good thing it's not a compound fracture or you'd have a nice case of blood poisoning from all the dirt. We'll put a plaster cast on it, and it'll be as good as new in three weeks. However, you won't be movin' very fast or far for a while. Got a place to stay?"

"No, sir. Been living at the mine 'til today."

"Maybe the Sisters can put you up until you're mobile." Marlow saw Sister Katherine give a nod from behind the physician. When finished with his inspection of Marlow, he asked, "What's your name, so I can make out this bill?"

"Hiram Marlow, sir."

The doctor handed the ten-dollar invoice to Marlow, who looked at it and said, "Doc, I don't have ten."

"How much you got?"

"About five," Marlow responded, wondering why in hell all the services in Ouray cost ten bucks, far more than he made in a week as a corporal.

"That'll do. I'm assuming the Sisters will provide you with board here until you're fit to get around on your own." Sister Katherine again nodded in the affirmative as the doctor moved on to inspect Rocco and then packed up his black bag. As he walked toward the door, he said to the Sister, "I need to keep going. We've got some disease down at the cribs."

Sister Katherine frowned. She'd had plenty of experience at the hospital with miners infected with venereal diseases.

"I thought the town said they'd mandate a monthly inspection of the girls?"

"Mayor complained that the town couldn't afford it even after I offered him my best price for individual inspections. Besides, the church ladies said an inspection would only encourage the girls to remain in Ouray. I wish there was a quick and easy solution for everyone's sake."

"The solution is simple," Sister Katherine said in a firm voice. "Outlaw prostitution. It's not only dirty but it's sinful."

"You need to talk with the town council," the doctor responded.

"I have. The problem is that half the bars in town are owned by two town council members. And, Doctor, you know as well as I that if the town was really serious about closing down prostitution, it'd be bad for local business, including your own."

The doctor smiled as he tipped his hat to Sister Katherine on his way out the door.

The hospital had a collection of old newspapers, which occupied Marlow's time for the first two days He found his small ward, which he shared with Rocco, bright and airy despite the sour smell of a strong disinfectant. The food, particularly the fresh meat and milk, was far superior to anything offered at the mine or the cantonment. He actually thought that after the first week he'd gained a pound or two. With the aid of a crutch, he could hop to the indoor bathroom, a real luxury. And he could feel the clavicle bone healing as the swelling diminished.

He found Sister Katherine and the other Sister helpful and attentive to his few needs. They took great pride in their work and explained to Marlow they had come over from Denver to establish the hospital a year and a half ago. Sister Katherine admitted the facility wasn't much to brag about. "But it is better than those wooden shacks they call 'infirmaries' up at the mines. We're planning a bigger and more modern hospital in about two years, after we raise the money. I wish the mine owners would be more generous," she said.

"I know what you mean." Marlow smiled.

Marlow felt cheered by the Sisters' presence, except when it came time for them to bathe him. His embarrassment never ceased, nor did it alter the Sisters' every-other-day routine of stripping him of his nightshirt.

Early one afternoon, Sister Katherine came to Marlow's bed with an official-looking letter from the Army adjutant general's office in Washington, addressed to Marlow at the Ouray Post Office, forwarded to the Columbine Mine, and then to the Miner's Hospital in Ouray, Colorado.

Not knowing anything about an adjutant general, Marlow wondered what the Army could want from him now.

To: Hiram Marlow, Private, 4th Cavalry Regiment, Uncompahgre Cantonment, Colorado

From: Headquarters, Adjutant General's Office, US Army, Washington, DC

December 10, 1881

At the request of Lt. General Philip Sheridan, Commander Military District of the Missouri, and by authority of General William T. Sherman, Commanding General of the United States Army, you are asked to provide, in the form of an affidavit, an account of what you witnessed on or about September 21, 1881, in Utah Territory with regard to Colonel Kindred and his treatment of sub-chief Running Bear of the Uncompahgre band of the Unified Tribe of the Ute.

You need to describe in your own words what you witnessed and any conversations you overheard or participated in that took place prior to or at the time of the shooting.

Your affidavit will be read by an Army Board of Inquiry, headed by Lt. General Philip Sheridan and appointed by General William T. Sherman to determine the seriousness of the charges made by Chief Shavano and others regarding Colonel Kindred's actions on the night of the shooting and the death of Running Bear.

By authority of the Adjutant General's Office you are hereby authorized to hire the services of a legal clerk at any county or district court in Colorado to assist you with this affidavit. The clerk will be reimbursed for his services.

/s/ Edward D. Townsend
Brigadier General,
Adjutant General, USA

Marlow dropped the letter onto the rough blankets. He rubbed his eyes with his good hand, and slid down off his pillow and under the covers to give thought to the general's letter.

Dolan was right about an investigation, Marlow thought. *I don't want to be involved in making trouble for Kindred, who seems the sort to make trouble for me the rest of my life. The letter "asks" me; now that I'm a civilian, they can't order me to provide information. Let those Army sons of bitches take care of their own problems. I'm honorably discharged; I don't owe them any damned favors after six years of service. If I write an affidavit relating the events of Kindred's cold-blooded murder of Running Bear, I'd have no future career in the Army, if, God forbid, I needed to reenlist, and certainly no favorable reference for a job outside the Army.*

But he couldn't forget the events of that morning when Kindred fired his pistol at Running Bear and a red mist, blood mixed with brain tissue and bone, sprayed from the exit cavity just above the Indian's ear. Marlow was revolted by the memory of that fucking martinet who wanted only to wear a star on his shoulder. *He thinks all Indians are savages*, Marlow thought. *But they are not. Not Bobby, who is like a brother to me back on the farm in Iowa. And certainly not Carroll, who I think of as a close friend. No, Kindred disgraced the government he represents and the uniform he wears. He looks at all Indians as if they were wild animals—like wolves—to be killed and a bounty to be collected. For Kindred, the bounty is his promotion. Maybe I should help whomever it is who wants to bring punishment to Kindred and justice to the Ute. Based on the accounts I've heard from Carroll, the Ute deserved a measure of justice from their "protectors." Yes, by God, I will write an affidavit about Kindred's murder and, if the colonel is brought before a firing squad, I'd even volunteer to be the one who puts the bullet between his eyes.*

SEVEN

OURAY, COLORADO

December 1881

The next morning when Sister Katherine came into the ward to shave and bathe him, Marlow asked, "Can you tell me about the importance of an affidavit?"

"Why do you ask?"

"Look at what I received from the Army yesterday." Marlow handed her the letter.

She read it. "This sounds serious to me. Were you involved in this killing?"

"Only as a witness. That's why the letter, I think. I may need some help. That's why I asked about an affidavit. Is there a certain format I need to follow? Certain things I should say or not say?"

"I really have no idea, but I know the clerk for the county judge. Maybe she could help," Sister Katherine suggested.

"She?"

"Yes, Mr. Marlow. Not all the hardworking Ouray girls are in the brothels . . . or hospitals."

"Could you ask her for me?"

"Better yet, I'll ask her to come to the hospital to meet with you and help with the affidavit."

"Thank you, Sister."

Waiting for the clerk, Marlow scratched notes to himself to refresh his memory. The more he thought about Kindred, the more agitated he became. Damn, he wanted to saw off the cast, get his shoulder out of the sling, and get on with his life. He was more than ready to forget about his Army service and mine employment.

The next day, Sister Katherine entered the ward accompanied by a young woman. "This is Sarah Platt, the clerk for the county judge. I think she can help you with that Army request."

Sarah's white teeth, surrounded by her full dark-pink lips, gave definition to her wide and generous smile. She leaned over Marlow and offered her small hand. As he reached for it, her aquamarine eyes shifted from his shaved face to his large, callused hand. She gave it a slight squeeze, to which he responded in kind and added a smile of his own. Marlow made an effort to sit higher up on the pillow, but his free arm slipped on the cotton sheet. The Sister reset the pillow, grabbed his free arm, and pulled while Marlow pushed himself backward with his good leg.

"That's more comfortable, thanks."

"How are your injuries doing?" Sarah asked.

"Healing," Marlow responded, looking at Sister Katherine. He turned toward Sarah and, after a short pause, added, "But all too slowly."

"He should be up and out of here in about a week," Katherine volunteered. "Now, let's hobble to my office where we can have some privacy," she suggested as she looked over at Rocco in his bed. Katherine helped pull Marlow out of bed and onto his good leg. He wrapped his free arm around Katherine's sturdy waist and together they made their way to her office, Sarah at his side. As much as Marlow disliked hopping along on one foot, the trip to the office with Sarah so close allowed him to take in her perfumed body, auburn hair, and slim figure. To extend the trip, Marlow suggested a detour outside.

"I'd love to get some fresh air and see the sun," Marlow said.

"I could help you outside for a minute or so," Sarah offered after Katherine gave an approving smile. She moved closer, taking Marlow's weight from the nun.

The two headed to the front door as Katherine walked to the doorway of her office.

"Don't let him fall, Sarah."

"I've got a good hold on him."

Marlow looked up at a brick house under construction across the street and then lifted his head to the snow-covered mountains. They reminded him of the mine and his accident.

"I'm glad to be out of those mountains and the dark, foul Columbine cave. Who wouldn't envy me now, being supported by a very attractive young lady?"

Sarah blushed.

"I think I'm going to fall," Marlow said.

Sarah grabbed him with both arms around his trunk. Marlow laughed as he rested his head on her shoulder.

Sarah unwrapped herself from Marlow and said in a playfully scolding tone, "I think you've had enough fresh air for now. Let's go back to Sister Katherine's office."

Once seated in the office, Sarah removed a notebook from her purse, and Katherine left them alone as she went off to perform her morning chores. "Now, about this military affidavit you've been asked to submit. I gather, from what Sister Katherine has told me, you were in the Army at the Uncompahgre Cantonment and were one of the soldiers who moved the Indians to Utah?"

"Correct."

"And it sounds like you witnessed an event involving Colonel Kindred's behavior that the Army is investigating?"

"Yes."

"All the Army wants is a statement, or affidavit, detailing what you witnessed that day. Your statement is part of an Army investigation to see if Colonel Kindred violated any Army orders or procedures. If he did, it is possible he will be brought up before a general court-martial."

"And if found guilty?" Marlow asked.

"I'm not familiar with military law, but I suspect he could be jailed, thrown out of the Army, maybe even shot or hanged."

"I'd offer to bring the rope."

"Apparently you dislike the colonel?"

"You bet I do," Marlow spit out.

"Remember, in the affidavit, you are only asked to provide facts, not opinions as to guilt or innocence."

"I understand, but, if the truth be known, the colonel's a cold-blooded murderer."

"That's for the Army court to decide, not a former private," Sarah declared.

Marlow didn't appreciate her response.

"I saw what I saw, and no law clerk is going to change my mind," Marlow spit out.

Sarah heard the anger in his voice and changed the focus of the discussion.

"I have a notepad here. Why don't you relate to me how the event unfolded, your duty that day, and how you came to be in the colonel's camp that morning? I may interrupt you from time to time to ask for some clarifying facts."

"OK, let's get to it," Marlow responded.

"All right then, tell me about the events leading up to your encounter with Colonel Kindred."

Marlow thought for a minute and then started his account of the day. Sarah took notes.

"As I remember, the day itself was uneventful. We'd ridden all day heading west in Utah, with no trouble from the Indians except for three or four who wanted to double back in search of a missing pony. That day I rode my young gelding to rest my other horse for guard duty. I had time for a little shut-eye after dinner so I'd be fresh for my shift starting at eleven. Our company was responsible for guarding the east perimeter of our encampment. Other units provided guards for the south, west, and north perimeters."

Marlow tried to think of all details that Sarah might question. He also wanted his affidavit to be as honest and complete as his memory would allow.

Marlow continued. "I had orders to keep a watch for any Indians or soldiers heading east and away from our encampment. Also I was to be alert to any civilians who might want to enter our encampment with trade items. Civilians who wished to enter our ranks had to show written permission from Colonel Kindred or District Headquarters in St. Louis." Marlow stopped and asked Sarah if he was speaking too fast for her to take notes. He hoped not. He wanted to finish this chore as quickly as possible so as to leave time for some personal conversation with this beautiful stenographer.

"Oh no, just keep going. You're doing fine. But one clarifying question: During your guard duty was there any moonlight?"

"Some, but not a full moon, maybe a half. Enough that I could make out the trees at the edge of the river and the mesas to the east and west outlined against the sky. Anyway, at what I guessed to be six in the morning, I heard a horse nicker off to my right."

As Sarah took businesslike notes, Marlow relaxed and recalled that morning. Marlow related his first encounter with Running Bear and his grisly discovery. He remembered his orders from Captain Griffin to take Running Bear to the colonel's headquarters. Then, with little regard for a lady's sensitivities, he opened up in graphic detail about Kindred's confrontations with Running Bear inside and outside his tent.

"That's a horrible story," Sarah said almost in a whisper. The soft scratch of her handwriting on the notepad paused, but she kept her eyes on the page.

"Yes, I wish that it would never have happened. I'll wake up in a sweat some nights dreaming about it. Murdering another human being for wanting to bury his mother . . . It makes no sense—none at all."

Marlow hesitated, then said, "I'd like to rest a minute if it's OK."

"Let's take a break and have that cup of tea that Sister Katherine left for us." Sarah raised her glance and gave a reassuring smile.

Marlow figured this might be an appropriate time to ask Sarah some questions of his own.

"What brought you to the town of Ouray?"

"My father is a merchant here. We moved here three years ago after my mother died of pneumonia back in Kansas City. I helped my dad in his hardware store until I hurt my back. Luckily I found a job as the clerk of the county court with the help of one of the county commissioners. The county sent me to Denver to learn shorthand, and I've been at the Ouray courthouse now for over a year. Nice job, but I sure prefer Denver to this place."

"Why so?"

"It gets pretty rough around here with all these miners. They're an unruly bunch, and dirty too. Work six days so they can get roaring drunk for twenty-four hours. Most of them are uncivilized, filthy, and crude in speech and behavior."

"Do you think I fit that category?"

"I hope not! You don't have those bloodshot, inquiring eyes or the tobacco-stained beard most of them have. Plus you're well spoken, I can tell."

"Well, it is only because the Sisters shave me every day. They take good care of me. They tell me I'll be ready to get out of here in a week or so. Then I'd like to take you to dinner. OK?"

"Sounds lovely, Mr. Marlow."

"Please, call me Hiram."

"Thank you, Hiram. Will you go back to the mine when you're well?"

"Not if I can help it. I'm not the type that enjoys working in a dark hole, even if they paid me all the money in China. But I'd like to stay around in these parts and make a decent wage. More money to be made here than in Iowa, my home. Any job ideas?"

"I just might have one. But I have to be getting back to the courthouse. See you at noon tomorrow and we can finish the affidavit." She stood up and squeezed Marlow's hand before her perfume evaporated through the doorway.

Marlow hobbled back to his ward, lay down on his cot, and fell immediately into a dream, with Sarah as the main subject.

The next day, Sunday, Sarah appeared in her church outfit—a full-length crimson wool dress, tight at the waist, and buttoned high up to her neck. She wore a small gold cross and had tied her long auburn hair into a neat bun atop her head. Marlow had never been in the presence of such a beautiful woman.

Sarah pulled out her pad and pencil. "Where were we? You had just witnessed the killing. Right?"

The question pulled Marlow out of his trance. He picked up Sarah's line of thought and continued. "Kindred had this big smile on his face as he came back into the tent. He ordered the duty officer to assemble a burial detail, and to summon Shavano. When the chief arrived he and Kindred engaged in a nasty shouting match. That about sums it up, Sarah."

Sarah had a few clarifying questions before she felt satisfied with the narrative flow of the affidavit. "Tomorrow, I'll write this up, then have you sign it and we'll send it off to Washington."

She placed the pad in her leather purse and continued. "You'll be having a guest here in a minute or so. It'll be my father. I've told him about you, the little I know about your Army background, your experience in the mine, and your hope of finding a job here in Ouray. Father has an opening at his hardware store for a clerk, and I said you might be the right person for that position. He wants to talk with you."

Marlow pulled himself higher up on his pillow and ran his fingers through his hair and across the old scabs on his forehead. "I must look like the devil. Hair uncombed, arm in a sling, leg in a cast. Who'd want to hire this cripple?"

Just as he finished his sentence, Sarah's father appeared in the ward. "Hiram, this is my father, Mr. Sidney Platt. Father, this is Hiram Marlow, who I've told you about," Sarah said.

The two men shook hands before Mr. Platt said, "I hope the Sisters are taking good care of you."

"Yes, sir, first class, unlike the Army or the Columbine Mine."

"I know the foreman up at the Columbine. Good operation, it is. If you want, I can see to it that you can have your job back after you're healed."

"Thanks, Mr. Platt, but I'm not a big fan of working in a dark hole, despite the pay. It's not the danger of the mine. It's that I like to work where the ceiling doesn't leak water and where the source of light is the sun, not a smoking candle."

"Did you finish high school?"

"Yes, sir, back in Iowa—with good grades. I wanted to go on to the agriculture college in Ames, but my father said I was needed on the farm."

"You can do arithmetic, I assume?"

"Yes, but I may be a little rusty. I've helped my mother with the farm accounts."

"You look like a sturdy lad to me. I can see strength in that good arm of yours, and if you worked as a mucker in the mines, you've a strong back. I'm looking for a clerk in my hardware store. The job involves hauling some heavy items off wagons and into the store, being knowledge-able about inventory and prices, and taking charge at the counter when I'm unavailable. You'd also have to make out sales receipts and clean the store after business on Saturday. I can pay you three fifty a day, with Sundays off. You can start when you're healed up from your injuries."

"I'd like that very much. Thank you, sir. The Sisters say I'll be out of my cast in about a week or so and also by then I should be able throw away the sling. I imagine it'll take me a few days to get my strength back and find lodging."

"How about you start on the first day of February?"

"Sounds good to me, Mr. Platt."

Sarah's smile reflected her pleasure with Marlow's decision.

EIGHT

WASHINGTON, DC

February 1882

General Philip Sheridan, Army commander of troops west of the Mississippi, hired a carriage at the Baltimore and Potomac rail station on Washington's Mall to take him to the War Department's building adjacent to the White House. He climbed the polished granite stairs to the front entrance, where two guards snapped off salutes to the three-star general.

One guard addressed Sheridan, "Sir, General Sherman is expecting you in his office. Go right at the first hallway; his office is at the end of the hall."

The size of the gray granite building still under construction impressed Sherman. The British had burned the old War Department building during the War of 1812. Though rebuilt, it became obsolete and crowded for the Army, Navy, and State Department. In the new larger building, not yet completed, the Army occupied the east wing.

Sheridan had looked forward to his Washington visit with his Civil War commander, whom he admired. The trip also broke the boredom of his command responsibilities for the Trans-Mississippi West, where he spent an inordinate amount of time traveling by rail, carriage, and horseback to inspect isolated and dreary Army posts from the Rio Grande in southern Texas to the Puget Sound in the Washington Territory. Walking down the hall of the new War Department building, Sheridan recognized Sherman's office by a white flag with four stars and a US flag hanging outside his door. A decorated Army master sergeant directed Sheridan into Sherman's smoke-filled private office. The general, with four bright gold stars on each shoulder board, rose from his chair behind the folder-laden desk, as his secretary excused himself.

"Phil, good to see you again. I'm most appreciative that you could come to Washington on such short notice. As you know, Senator McCabe moved the date of our budget appropriations session up by two weeks. I need you at that hearing. Also we have some other matters to discuss. But first, how was your trip?"

"The trip from Chicago went well except for the food. Horrible. The New York Central must buy it from the Navy." Both generals laughed.

"We're about to go into a meeting with my senior staff. You'll know the members."

Sherman led the way into an adjoining conference room where Sheridan recognized the two generals responsible for planning and quartermaster supplies, respectively. The two other senior officers in attendance headed troop training and recruitment.

Sherman led off a discussion about supply shortages hindering the Army's effectiveness, especially on the frontier.

"To briefly review our situation, Congress cut the size of the Army after the war to thirty thousand. Ten years later our size was twenty-seven thousand. Then with General Custer's defeat, Congress boosted our manpower to thirty-seven thousand, which still leaves us spread dangerously thin throughout the West. We don't have the troops to fulfill our mission on the western frontier, which is to provide security for the railroad construction crews, protect the overland emigrant trails, and kill and destroy all hostile Indians while keeping other Indians on their reservations, separated from whites. That's why I've had to create three Negro regiments. With our pay scales what they are, it seems that only Negroes want to join the Army. Our current problem is money for salaries, equipment, supplies, and ammunition. I want this to be the focus of our testimony before both the House and Senate committees."

Sherman turned to his quartermaster general. "General Mcigs, you might want to add a word here."

"Thank you, General. Supply shortages exist throughout the Army regardless of unit or location. I know on the western frontier it is particularly critical. For instance, Colonel Kindred of the 4th Cavalry, before he was relieved of his command a month ago, sent me letters almost weekly complaining about the poor quality of food and the lack of proper clothing for his troops. He blamed the inadequacies for his regiment's high desertion rate. Poor provisions become a cause of poor health. 'When scurvy and cholera appear, desertion becomes a popular antidote,' to quote from a Kindred letter. Without an adequate appropriation, I found it impossible to fulfill Kindred's reasonable requests or similar ones from other commanders."

The general looked at his notes and continued. "While on the subject of Kindred, I'm sorry to say it, but Kindred made a number of unreasonable requests also. After I sent him a hundred fifty buffalo winter coats as he requested, he wanted three hundred fifty more a month later. I sent him seventy new carbines, and then he wanted an additional fifty. Do they eat them out there on the frontier? Or maybe they hand 'em to the redskins. I don't wish to single out Colonel Kindred. There are a number of other regimental commanders I could name. But sir, they all need additional or replacement equipment and better food."

The discussion went on into early evening when Sherman called an adjournment. "We'll break for dinner and reconvene tomorrow at two o'clock in the afternoon. I want to discuss some promotions, plus a confidential matter."

As the others gathered their notes, Sherman asked, "Phil, can you join me for supper at the Willard?"

"Wish I could, General, but I'm committed to eating with my in-laws with whom I'm staying in Georgetown. I need to convince them that Chicago is safe from Indian attacks."

★   ★   ★

The next afternoon, the group gathered in Sherman's conference room. The white walls served as a background for six colorful battle flags and a large map of the United States with over a hundred pins designating Army installations. The men sat around the heavy wooden table. The general briefly consulted his notes.

"General Tillman Bishop, the commander of the 3rd Infantry Division, retires next month, and his replacement must be recommended to the president and the Senate. As many of you might guess, because he always applies for a general's billet when one becomes vacant, I have a letter from Colonel Joseph Kindred, of the 4th Cavalry, dated before he was relieved of his command, requesting appointment to the rank of brigadier and reassignment to the 3rd Infantry. Kindred cites his senior status as a colonel, his Civil War record, including his command of an infantry regiment and his victories against six Indian tribes on the western and southern frontiers. As much as I admire Kindred's combat record, I must say I am not impressed with the tone of his letter. He makes it sound as if he's entitled to the promotion. The letter borders on making a demand rather than a request."

Sherman continued. "We also have another problem with Kindred. As some of you know, he commanded the 2nd Connecticut Heavy Artillery Regiment during a period of the war. Senator McCabe served as a captain in that unit. To this day, he blames Kindred for the unit's excessive losses at Antietam and constantly refers to Kindred in public as an 'incompetent prima donna.' I need not remind you that Senator McCabe is chairman of the Military Appropriations Committee with whom we must make our appearance next week.

"Also I need to inform you of a very unfavorable investigation regarding Kindred's recent behavior in Colorado. I cannot, therefore, recommend Kindred for the vacancy. Instead I'd like to recommend Colonel John Kerr to the president for the general's billet." Sherman's staff nodded quietly almost in unison.

"I'm uncertain if Mr. Arthur, our new president, will accept my recommendation. As you may have heard, just last week the president made his own independent decision on some other Army promotions I had suggested to him. His appointments, no doubt, were influenced by the president's close ally and supporter, Senator Conkling of New York. I understand nothing will get done in this administration, including the president's desire for civil service reform, unless it has the blessing of Conkling."

All the men agreed with the commanding general's recommendations, as well as his opinions about Kindred and the new president.

Sherman then proceeded to describe Sheridan's investigation regarding Kindred's indefensible action against Running Bear, a Ute sub-chief. He specially made reference to two affidavits, including Marlow's. Sherman made it clear that the preliminary investigation uncovered enough information about the killing of Running Bear and Kindred's total disregard of General Sheridan's order to "move and protect" the Ute to warrant a court-martial. He read Shavano's letter verbatim with its not-so-subtle threat of trouble unless Kindred was brought to justice. The threat of trouble captured the staff's full attention.

Sherman pointed to a stack of letters he'd received after the Sheridan confidential investigative report was made public by the *New York Herald*. Some liberal Republican senators who called themselves "friends to the Indians" had written the president to criticize Kindred and the Army. The *Hartford Courant* quoted Senator McCabe as calling for punishment of "the undisciplined." And editorials in Philadelphia, New York, and Boston newspapers also urged the Army to immediately court-martial the colonel.

Sherman summed up his presentation of the Kindred incident. "From what I have read, particularly in the affidavits I have assembled, it seems to me Kindred has injured the Army's reputation. The public and key members of Congress, particularly Senator McCabe, believe we have much to account for. And then there are other damned senators who are investigating our contracts with suppliers, particularly weapons manufacturers. The president too is displeased about Kindred's behavior, after reading General Sheridan's report." Sherman stopped, stomped out his cigar on the floor, and, as his eyes narrowed, said in an angry voice, "That goddamned colonel doesn't know how to follow a simple order."

The staff sat silent, staring at Sherman.

The general broke the silence. "Your thoughts, gentlemen."

"Why must the Army bring him to trial?" the colonel in charge of Army recruitment asked. "I believe there is a law outlawing murder of an Indian by a white man. Let the civil courts deal with him, and we can stay out of it."

Sherman responded. "You're correct about the law. The problem is that the crime occurred in Utah Territory. There's not a goddamned official in the territory, especially a Mormon, who'd charge a white man with killing an Indian."

Another general at the table advised caution. A court-martial proceeding against an active-duty colonel would create definite morale problems within the senior officer ranks of the Army. "Given our treatment by Congress over the past fifteen years, especially the pay scale for commissioned and non-commissioned officers, it is my observation that the Army's morale has never been lower. A court-martial of a well-known and successful colonel will not sit well with our soldiers or officers. I'd expect more resignations and desertions."

Meigs, the quartermaster general, stood up from the end of the conference table. "By all means, gentlemen, let us be realistic here. If we fail to bring a court-martial against Kindred for his damned foolish actions, you can be sure that Senator McCabe will take another bite out of our ass. Must we protect a colonel whose actions, at least from what I have heard, appear indefensible? Our morale is not weak. It is our reputation that is under attack."

Another officer asked Sherman, "Sir, what would Kindred be charged with in the court-martial? Certainly not with killing an Indian."

"Killing an Indian, no. That is part of our Army mission. Nor is the issue the brutal manner in which Kindred killed the sub-chief—tied his hands behind his back and shot him point-blank in the temple, although that's certainly not an honorable way for a United States Army colonel to conduct himself. We don't court-martial soldiers for the manner in which they kill their enemy, though you might remember the Army wanted to court-martial Colonel Chivington, the Colorado Methodist minister who raised two volunteer cavalry regiments before he massacred and mutilated some peaceful Indians at Sand Creek. Chivington cleverly avoided the court-martial proceedings by resigning before the court could convene.

"No, the issue before us is not one of rank or the manner of killing, or placating Senator McCabe, but military regulations. As I see it, the colonel violated the orders given to him by General Sheridan. Those orders specified that he was 'to protect' Chief Shavano's Ute band as it moved from the Uncompahgre Valley in southwest Colorado to the Ute's new reservation in Utah. General

Sheridan, with my approval, also authorized the colonel to use whatever force he deemed necessary to carry out this mission. Personally, I believe Kindred stretched that authority too far and should be brought before a military court for failure to follow orders. That is, he failed to protect the sub-chief. Whether the colonel needed to kill the sub-chief to protect Shavano's band, I leave that decision to the court. It would be ironic, would it not, if the court agreed that the sub-chief needed to be murdered or, if you prefer, killed, to protect the band. In my orders to Kindred I intentionally included the word 'protect,' and that does not usually entail point-blank shots to the head."

He turned to Sheridan. "Phil, do you have anything you wish to add?"

"Sir, I am in agreement with what you say. But, like General Meigs, I am also concerned about Army morale if Kindred is found guilty. Colonel Kindred is probably our most renowned Indian fighter, a commander who adheres to our 'total war' concept. Look what he did against the Comanche in Texas and some of the northern tribes in Montana. Kindred learned quickly, by personal experience, that you don't defeat Indians using the tactics currently taught in our military schools. No, you must use unconventional methods against an unconventional enemy.

"Let's be honest here: Kindred knows how to fight Indians and now we are thinking about bringing the colonel before a court-martial board. Is the Army strong enough to survive what would be a temporary embarrassment? Probably, but there is no doubt our reputation before the public and Congress will be weakened. They will say we are hypocrites. We promote a successful Indian fighter and then punish him for killing Indians. On the other hand, what will be the reaction of Senator McCabe if we don't press charges against Kindred? And what if a military court finds Kindred totally innocent of those charges?"

Sherman responded, "We shouldn't worry about the court's decision. The adjutant general tells me he has a strong case against Kindred. Yes, we may be looked upon by some as hypocritical but our appropriation request and Senator McCabe's support is all-important. The president has asked that I brief him on this issue. I will recommend that a court-martial of Colonel Kindred go forward. In the end, given the political pressures, it is the president's decision to approve a court-martial or let the issue drop. Of course, whatever his decision, we will support it.

"Phil, I know you are not in full agreement with my decision, but the Army will survive this mess."

Sheridan responded. "The dumb son of a bitch disobeyed a direct order. That is cause enough for me to bring Kindred to trial."

"Thank you, Phil. I'd like you to continue to meet with my staff here and get you prepared for the hearings next week. The comptroller has all the necessary figures on expenditures. I'll be here in my office for the rest of the week with the exception of a troop review at Fort Monroe on Thursday. Also the president's office tells me there will be a Crow chief here in town Friday. I suspect I'll have to do my best Indian dance with him and take him out to Fort Belvoir for a Gatling-gun demonstration. Since Custer's death, I've instituted these demonstrations to shock the Indian chiefs. They never fail to impress, if not intimidate, the Indians . . . makes them think twice about engaging us in battle. We are dismissed."

The officers came to attention around the table and saluted in unison. Sherman returned the salute, brushed the ashes from his old cigar off his blue uniform, lit a new one, and returned to his desk with the same scowl he wore when he began the meeting.

The next morning Sherman interrupted Sheridan's work with the senior staff. "Phil, we have an appointment with the president in thirty minutes. He wants to talk about the Kindred matter and some other Army appointments."

The two generals walked out the back door of the War Department building and across the lawn to the White House staff entrance. A Marine guard halted the two generals, requested identification, and, once satisfied, saluted the senior officers. A valet led Sherman and Sheridan through a noisy crowd of office-seekers, who were making their headquarters in the chairs and on the floor of the Blue Room, waiting to see President Chester Arthur, who had assumed the presidency a month earlier after the assassination of President James Garfield.

Arthur sat at his desk, which was piled with folders and reports prepared for him by an inherited cabinet, which remained wary of the new president's leadership qualities. The president's mutton-chop whiskers covered his jowls and most of his mouth so that when he spoke it appeared as if his words emerged from a thicket of dead brown weeds.

"Good morning, generals. General Sheridan, I haven't seen you since my visit to Chicago earlier this year. Very good to see you again, and welcome to Washington."

"Mr. President, it's always a pleasure to visit Washington and to see General Sherman."

"The newspapers continue to commend you for your success in the West. Very dirty business, I'm sure. And

General Sherman, I know you requested this meeting to discuss a very sensitive court-martial. Please sit down, gentlemen. There's a pot of coffee over by the window beneath the portrait of Jefferson. I'm still overwhelmed by the paperwork that has accumulated since President Garfield's assassination. What a terrible deed. All my time right now is focused on assembling a new cabinet and keeping thousands of office-seekers at bay. Thankfully, I don't have to worry about the Army's leadership. To you, General Sherman, I am much in debt and appreciative of your support, especially after your brother lost my party's nomination to President Garfield."

"Thank you, Mr. President. I am assisted by superb senior officers like General Sheridan, and I like to believe that politics do not enter into my military conduct."

"Yes, by all means. Now let us discuss this court-martial matter. It has, as you know, attracted considerable attention in the newspapers. Also there are some very important political implications."

Sherman outlined the Kindred situation, reading both Shavano's letter and parts of Marlow's affidavit from Sheridan's investigative report. He presented the pros and cons of proceeding with a court-martial.

"Not a pretty situation," the president responded, "especially with Congress. Their current investigation of Army contracts is certain to hurt you, regardless of the outcome, and that son-of-a-bitch McCabe is lying in the grass just waiting to strike the Army and the Navy, all the while making tariff threats against some of our European friends. I don't know what the man is thinking, but he can be a pain in the ass. Still, we have to work with him, maybe even placate him, if I am to have any support from the reform wing of the Republican Party.

"After reading those two affidavits and your orders to Kindred, my feeling is we should go ahead with the court-martial. But we should go easy on him. We don't want to stir up any more hornets. If it can be arranged, just get through the trial with the least amount of damage to the Army, and give Kindred a slap on the wrist. Sure, the Indian reformers will scream like hell, but at least we responded to their call for justice. Also I'm concerned by Shavano's letter and his threat of an Indian uprising. I sure as hell don't need an Indian war on my hands, and it sounds to me like Shavano has the means to start one. General Sherman, do you have reservations about proceeding with a court-martial?"

Ever since the investigation of Kindred, Sherman had given considerable thought to the appropriateness of a court-martial. He had learned over the two decades of his military career it was the Army as an organization, not the individuals within Army ranks, that demanded loyalty. The commanding general of the Army would not admit it publicly, not even to his senior staff, but the survival and future strength of the entire Army remained more important to Sherman than the career of a single officer. By recommending the court-martial of Kindred, Sherman's decision suggested that he was willing to sacrifice the career of a senior officer in return for the preservation of a combat-ready Army. The Army needed Senator McCabe's goodwill and support for appropriations. If Kindred had to serve as the sacrificial lamb for the politicians and the press, so be it.

"No reservations, Mr. President."

"And you, General Sheridan?"

Sheridan hesitated a few seconds and responded, "I agree with General Sherman."

"Good, then let's move with all due speed. I'll get a letter off to Shavano with the news."

"Sir, we will proceed with the court-martial as soon as possible," Sherman said.

The two generals returned to Sherman's office. Sherman lit a fresh cigar and said to Sheridan, "I think the court should sit at Fort Leavenworth, as far away from the liberal eastern press as possible. I'd like to see General Miles, an Indian fighter himself, as the presiding officer of the court. I believe Miles can keep the trial under control so as not to embarrass the Army, nor add fuel to McCabe's animus.

"General Crook should also be on the court. Like Miles, he knows about fighting Indians. I could use your recommendation for the third general to sit with them. I know Miles is no fan of Kindred, but he's run military trials before, and I can ask him to go easy on Kindred. I'll also ask Adjutant General Townsend to assign Kindred a top-notch defense counsel. I hate like hell to make it a precedent of court-martialing an active-duty colonel, but it appears we have no choice. We don't need approval from Mr. Lincoln, the secretary of war, but I'll keep him informed. I'm sure I can convince him of the need for the court-martial.

"Now, how goes preparation for the congressional hearings?" Sherman asked.

"Expect a doubling of our appropriations," Sheridan said with a wide smile. Sherman's scowl remained.

NINE

March 1882

"The court will come to order," General Miles announced to the crowded courtroom at Fort Leavenworth. The Army's largest garrison west of the Mississippi River served as a convenient location for an Army court-martial, as much for its geographical location as for the presence of the Army's high-security prison, an imposing brick-and-stone structure standing alone in the middle of the garrison. Over the years, the post's soldiers provided security for the Santa Fe Trail and manpower for the wars against the Plains Indians. On a normal training day, a visitor could hear the explosion of artillery shells, the crisp pop of carbine shots, and the hoofbeats of cavalry horses maneuvering into formations on the hard-clay parade ground.

"I am authorized by General William Sherman, commander in chief of the United States Army, General Order

#62, to convene this court for the purpose of determin-
ing the innocence or guilt of Colonel Joseph P. Kindred,
United States Army. Colonel Kindred is charged by the
Army for disobeying a direct order from General Philip
Sheridan on September 21, 1881, in the Utah Territory."
Miles introduced the two other generals sitting with him
at the table in their dress blue uniforms covered with campaign ribbons. The defense counsel, Captain Chapin from
the adjutant general's office, and Kindred sat at a table facing the three generals. Kindred also wore his dress blues
with the gold spread eagle insignia on each shoulder. He
hid his right hand under his left arm. At another table sat
the prosecuting officer, Colonel Peters, and his assistant. A
civilian court stenographer sat off to the side by an armed
military guard.

Hiram Marlow, in a coat and tie; Ben Carroll, wearing
a beaded buckskin shirt; and Captain Olson, in his dress
blue uniform, sat together in the first row of seats reserved
for witnesses who would be called to the stand. Other
seats were occupied by officers from the adjutant general's
office and the press, including the *New York Tribune* and
Philadelphia Inquirer.

"The Army will state its case against Colonel Joseph
P. Kindred," Miles said to the Army prosecutor, and then
took a dip of snuff.

Colonel Peters, in his dress blues with three rows
of campaign ribbons, stepped in front of his desk and
declared, "It is the Army's intent to show that Colonel
Kindred, on September 21, 1881, in the Territory of Utah,
failed to follow orders from General Philip Sheridan when
Colonel Kindred killed Running Bear, a sub-chief of Chief
Shavano's Uncompahgre Ute band. General Sheridan had
given very specific orders to protect the Ute during their

move from their Colorado reservation to a new reservation in the Utah Territory. The Army contends that when
Colonel Kindred killed Running Bear, he failed to protect
the sub-chief and, by his actions, failed to follow orders."

Kindred gave his full attention to Colonel Peters.
Marlow showed a small smile as he heard for the first time
about General's Sheridan's specific order.

"It will be asserted by the defense counsel that the
colonel had good reason to take excessive action against
Running Bear. The sub-chief had, earlier the day before
on September 20, 1881, come to the general's headquarters with his uncle, Chief Shavano, to ask permission to
return to Colorado with the corpse of his mother. It is an
Indian custom that her body be placed with her deceased
relatives—in this case, in a cave near the Los Piños Indian
Agency in the Uncompahgre Valley. In his affidavit to
this court, Mr. Carroll, the interpreter who was present
at the meeting, reported that the colonel turned down the
request. The following day, after Running Bear's capture
by Corporal Marlow, the colonel screamed at Running
Bear—I quote from Mr. Carroll's affidavit—'We will bury
your mother or place her in a tree for the vultures to feast
on, but she is not going with us to Utah.'"

Kindred sneered at Colonel Peters while the press
scribbled furiously to keep up with the fast-moving
testimony.

"Mr. Carroll added that in the same meeting the colonel referred to Running Bear as, and again I quote from
Mr. Carroll's affidavit, 'a red son of a bitch.' Officers of the
court, I know it is hard to imagine, but this is the foul language used by an Army colonel representing the United
States!"

Captain Chapin quickly stood up as if ready to make an objection. He said nothing and then took his seat as General Miles glared at him.

Immediately Miles interrupted the proceedings. "Will the interpreter be called as a witness?"

"Yes, sir."

"Proceed, Colonel."

"At this point I'd like to call to the witness stand Mr. Hiram Marlow, a former corporal in C Company of the 4th Cavalry, who stood guard through the night of September 20."

Marlow stepped from the front row and took a seat in the witness chair after being sworn in by Miles. He wiped perspiration from his brow with the sleeve of his new wool suit.

The prosecuting counsel addressed the ex-soldier. "Mr. Marlow, please state for the court your orders as a guard on the night of September 20 and the events which occurred early the morning of September 21."

"Sir, as you mentioned, I pulled guard duty the evening of September 20, and I'd been given the same orders as all the other guards: to ensure that no one, soldier or Indian, in the encampment be allowed to leave the boundaries without the signed permission of a company commander or Colonel Kindred's adjutant. I was also ordered to prevent entry to our military encampment by any unauthorized civilians."

Peters interrupted the testimony and asked Marlow, "Why did your orders include protection against 'unauthorized civilians'?"

"Sir, we understood the Mormons were not pleased about the Colorado Ute being resettled in their territory and being given a new reservation near some Mormon communities. Our company commander informed us that there was a possibility of Mormons sneaking into our encampment and killing Indians. There was also the possibility that civilian merchants might come in to sell weapons, ammunition, and liquor to the Ute."

"I assume you were authorized to use force if a Ute attempted to leave the encampment?" Peters asked.

"If the Ute did not have permission to leave and refused to return to the encampment on my signal, I was ordered to shoot him," Marlow responded.

"And who issued that order?"

"Colonel Kindred," Marlow said.

"Continue your testimony, Mr. Marlow."

"Early the next morning of September 21, probably about six o'clock, I heard a horse nicker off to the north. It had probably smelled my horse from a distance. I rode over in the direction of the noise and could see in the dawn's light the outline of a horse and rider. I galloped fast to intercept their movement. I pulled my pistol as I came upon the rider, an Indian, with his horse dragging a travois. I signaled for the Indian to stop and dismount, and he did. I inspected the travois, and it contained a long canvas package wrapped in hide strips. I unfolded one end to discover it was a dead squaw woman, a relative, I assumed. In sign language I told the Indian to follow me on horseback. We rode to C Company headquarters where I related to my company commander, Captain Griffin, the attempted escape of the Indian. I was then ordered to tie the Indian's hands behind his back and lead him and his travois to Colonel Kindred's headquarters.

"The colonel's tent was lit by a lamp so that I could see the duty officer, Captain Olson, sitting outside the tent. I saluted; gave my name, rank, and company; and proceeded to relate my orders from Captain Griffin. Captain Olson entered Colonel Kindred's tent, and within minutes Colonel Kindred stepped outside. The colonel ordered the captain to find Mr. Carroll, the interpreter, and bring him to the command post.

"The colonel demanded to know why I had taken an Indian prisoner. He reminded me that before our departure from the Uncompahgre Valley, the colonel had ordered that soldiers not take any Indian prisoners but to shoot if we thought the Indian was trying to escape our military command. I told the colonel that because the Indian was dragging a travois with his dead mother, he might have permission to do so. I didn't want to kill an Indian who, I thought, probably had permission to bury his mother back in Uncompahgre Valley."

Colonel Peters interrupted Marlow. "Upon what basis did you make that assumption, Corporal? Your orders were very specific: take no prisoners. Did you assume that the colonel or another senior officer had cancelled the order about prisoners?"

"No, sir," Marlow continued in a calm manner. "Again, I was uncertain if the Indian had permission to return to his home."

"If the Indian had permission to return to Colorado, wouldn't you have been told before guard duty about this situation? And wouldn't the Indian have been accompanied by a soldier who would have informed you that the Indian had permission to exit your camp?"

"Not necessarily, sir. He might have been carrying a note signed by the colonel or a senior officer. In this situation, Running Bear did not show me a note. Also, if the Indian was intent on escaping, he'd be in a fast gallop not a slow walk. It was then that I became curious about the contents of his travois."

"Continue on, Mr. Marlow," General Miles ordered.

Marlow went on to detail the colonel's questioning of the captured Indian, whose hands had been untied per Kindred's orders. "The colonel recognized the Indian as the one who, with Shavano, had asked the colonel the day before for permission to return to the Colorado reservation with his deceased mother. The Ute wanted to place her in a cave with other family members. The colonel reminded Running Bear he had turned down his earlier request. Then the colonel started screaming at the Indian, insulting him and his mother, calling them savages, and ordering the Indian to get rid of her corpse. I don't know if Mr. Carroll gave a word-for-word interpretation, but, like a mountain lion, Running Bear sprang at the colonel, tackled him to the ground, and tried to strangle him." The judges leaned forward, looking surprised by the testimony.

Then facing Kindred, Marlow said, "If not for my efforts and those of Mr. Carroll and the duty officer, the colonel's life might have ended right there on the dirt floor of his tent."

Marlow took a deep breath and continued. "As the colonel staggered to his feet, he reached over to the chair by his cot and picked up his holstered pistol. With his pistol in hand, he ordered me to tie the hands of Running Bear behind his back and take him outside. I did as I was ordered.

"Kindred next ordered me to force Running Bear to his knees, and then ordered me and the interpreter to go back inside the tent to join the duty officer. Through the tent's half-open flap I could see outside where the colonel stood over the Indian. The colonel leaned over Running

Bear, spit in his face, slapped him, and called him a dirty, filthy savage. Then the colonel pulled a pistol from his holster and put the weapon to the Indian's head, right behind his ear. The general cocked the hammer with both hands and pulled the trigger. Running Bear fell to the ground and lay motionless in a pool of blood."

As soon as Marlow paused in his testimony, Kindred stood up and shouted, "The Army's mission is to kill Indians! I killed that savage in my line of duty!"

General Miles responded immediately to Kindred's outburst. "The colonel is out of order and will take his seat."

"The hell I am. I won't sit here and listen to lies. This is my career at stake, and I won't have it destroyed by a soldier I once had to break in rank for disobeying my direct order."

General Miles immediately rose from his chair and pointed angrily at Kindred. "Colonel, you are out of order. If you do not sit down and remain quiet, I will have you removed from these proceedings. You and your defense counsel will have an opportunity to cross-examine any and all witnesses before this court. Do I make myself clear, Colonel?"

Kindred nodded to General Miles, turned to Marlow with an angry look, and took his seat.

"Proceed, Mr. Marlow," General Miles ordered.

Unnerved by Kindred's outbreak before a court of general officers and Miles's reprimand, Marlow tried to calm his nerves and keep focused on his testimony. Marlow took another deep breath and continued. "The colonel called for Chief Shavano, who arrived shortly at the colonel's headquarters. Through Mr. Carroll, the interpreter, Colonel Kindred explained to the chief the circumstances of the argument with Shavano's nephew, Running Bear, how he had disobeyed the colonel's order issued in Shavano's presence, and that the colonel had to kill Running Bear in self-defense in their recent encounter. Shavano stood shaking as he looked first at Mr. Carroll and then at Colonel Kindred."

Peters interrupted. "Mr. Marlow, you said that the colonel explained his actions as 'self-defense.' Is that correct?"

"Yes, sir."

"How could Running Bear be a physical threat to the colonel if he was on his knees with his hands tied behind his back?"

"I don't know, sir."

The defense counsel, Captain Chapin, interrupted. "Running Bear had already threatened the colonel's life."

"Yes, but not when his hands were tied behind his back," Peters countered.

Chapin did not respond.

"Continue on, Mr. Marlow," General Miles directed the witness.

"Chief Shavano appeared angered by what he'd heard from the colonel. He asked Carroll again for an interpretation. Then Shavano turned to the colonel and asked under what authority did he kill his nephew and then have him buried with his sister. He also challenged the colonel's claim that the Uncompahgre Ute were under military authority. The Ute had not, he said, signed any agreement or treaty to that effect. He said the government asked them to move to Utah, and they agreed to the move by signing the Peace Treaty. And, as an act of good faith, Shavano said, his warriors gave up their arms without a struggle for the duration of the move, making them defenseless against the colonel's temper. He ended his confrontation with the colonel by saying that if an Indian treated a senior Army officer the way the colonel treated Running Bear, the Indian would be shot on sight. And then Shavano shouted in English: '*We demand justice, Colonel!*'

"Colonel Kindred had no more to say, and to conclude the meeting, offered his hand. Shavano refused it. Instead the chief tore his Presidential Peace Medal from his neck, threw it on the ground, stomped on it, and left. The colonel swore at Shavano and called him back. Shavano paid no attention as he mounted his horse and rode away. Having no other business with the colonel, I exited the command post and returned to my company headquarters."

Peters asked, "Did you report to your company commander the conversation between the colonel and Chief Shavano?"

"No, sir, I did not."

"And why not, Mr. Marlow?"

"Captain Griffin did not ask for a report. Also I feared retribution from the colonel had I volunteered the details of Running Bear's killing."

Captain Chapin rose and asked permission to cross-examine Marlow.

"Mr. Marlow, it is a known fact that among the enlisted men and officers of your cavalry company at the Uncompahgre Cantonment you were considered a friend of the Ute. You would visit their lodges on Sundays and trade with them. Is this true?"

"One lodge, yes, sir."

"And that you were a friend of the Indian interpreter, Mr. Carroll?"

"Yes, sir. Is there something wrong with that?"

"Mr. Marlow, may I remind you that I'm the one asking the questions in a cross-examination, not the witness."

General Miles spoke up. "Mr. Marlow, Captain Chapin is correct. But Captain, I don't understand why Marlow's friendship with Indians has any bearing in this case."

Chapin continued. "Sir, I'm suggesting that Marlow's friendship with Indians has biased his testimony against Colonel Kindred, a well-known Indian fighter."

Peters asked General Miles for permission to address this issue at this time in the proceedings.

"Proceed, Colonel Peters."

"The defense has presented no evidence to the court that Mr. Marlow's so-called friendship with the Ute extended beyond a single family or that his friendship with the Indian interpreter influenced his testimony in any way. Such an argument, I would suggest to the court, makes no rational sense. It is only an opinion of the defense."

The court appeared to agree with Peters's comment. Miles told Chapin to continue his cross-examination.

"Marlow, how could you have found Colonel Kindred's headquarters in the dark?"

"Sir, it was early dawn with enough light for me to locate the colonel's headquarters."

"At a quarter after six in the morning, as you stated?"

"That's an estimate, Captain. It may have been later."

"Or earlier?" the captain added without waiting for an answer. "You testified that you first made contact with the duty officer, who notified the colonel of your presence and the reason for your presence at such an early hour."

"That is correct, sir."

"Also you testified that when you brought Running Bear into the colonel's tent, you were ordered to untie the chief's hands. Who ordered you to untie his hands?"

"Colonel Kindred."

"And then the Indian charged the colonel, is that correct?"

"Yes, sir, but only after the colonel insulted the Indian."

"Mr. Marlow, that wasn't my question. And I'd remind the court that the witness has no authority to give his opinion as to motives. I ask that the last statement be stricken from the record."

Colonel Peters rose and objected. "Mr. Marlow is not offering an opinion but a description of events. In his affidavit it is clear that the colonel's words to Running Bear agitated the sub-chief."

General Miles allowed Marlow's statement to remain in the record. "Continue with your cross-examination, Captain Chapin."

"Mr. Marlow, in your testimony you state that after Colonel Kindred was viciously attacked by Running Bear, he picked himself up from the ground with your help and reached for his pistol, which was, I assume, holstered and attached to a belt of some type, and hanging somewhere nearby the colonel's bunk. Correct?"

"Yes, sir."

"Can you identify the make and model of the pistol for the court?"

"It looked to me to be a standard military service revolver, a Colt forty-five caliber, except it had a pearl handle . . . Not standard military issue, as far as I know."

"Again I want to remind the court you're once more offering an opinion like much of the rest of your testimony."

Peters stood up and objected. "This is not an opinion but a statement of fact. The pistol had a pearl handle, which is *not* standard on an Army pistol, even for a colonel."

The cross-examination continued. "In your affidavit you state that the colonel ordered you to take Running Bear outside the colonel's tent. Correct?"

"Yes, sir, I retied Running Bear's hands behind his back and pushed him outside. The colonel followed behind me. Then he ordered me to force Running Bear to his knees and return to the tent."

"How could you possibly witness the events you describe in your affidavit—the colonel spitting in Running Bear's face, the name calling, and then the shooting of Running Bear—when, in fact, you were inside the tent?"

"Mr. Carroll, Captain Olson and I witnessed the events through the open flap in the tent, as I described in my affidavit."

"Even though he had his hands tied, how can you be certain that Running Bear did not make a threatening move toward the colonel?"

"I did not see or hear any such threat."

"But again, you are witnessing these events through a half-open tent flap. Correct?"

"Sir, it was more than half-open."

"But not fully so. Is that not true?"

"Yes, sir."

"Isn't it possible that Running Bear said something to threaten Colonel Kindred?"

"Sir, I did not hear Running Bear say anything to the colonel."

"Because you were too far away to hear?"

"No, sir. Both Running Bear and the colonel were standing right outside the tent about fifteen feet from where we stood inside the tent."

Captain Chapin continued his cross-examination. "Would you say that the colonel was nervous or agitated in his confrontation with Running Bear outside the tent?"

"Definitely."

"I would suggest to the court that Colonel Kindred had reason to be agitated. Running Bear had already attacked him in the tent and made a move to do so again when outside the tent. The colonel shot Running Bear in self-defense, clear and simple."

Colonel Peters rose again and asked for permission to speak.

"The defense would have us believe that this famous Indian fighter, Colonel Kindred, could be threatened by an Indian who is on his knees with his hands tied behind his back. From Mr. Marlow's affidavit, we know that Running Bear offered no resistance at the moment when Colonel Kindred pulled the trigger to blow his brains out. Officers of the court, Colonel Kindred dishonored the US Army by his action and deserves punishment from this court in the same way that Colonel Chivington, who massacred Indians at Sand Creek, was condemned by a congressional committee. I quote from their Chivington court report: 'for the purpose of vindicating the cause of justice and upholding the honor of the nation, prompt and energetic measures should be at once taken to remove from office those who have thus disgraced the government . . . and to punish, as their crimes deserve, those who have been guilty of these brutal and cowardly acts.'

"You know and God knows that Colonel Kindred committed a brutal and cowardly act. I repeat again, he deserves punishment from this court."

Captain Chapin rose instantly to object.

"I want to remind the court that this trial is not about Colonel Chivington and what he may or may not have done to the Indians at Sand Creek almost twenty years ago. This is about Colonel Kindred, whose honorable and distinguished military career is known to every senior officer in the US Army. I submit for the record two letters of commendation for Colonel Kindred. One letter from General U. S. Grant, dated August of 1865, commends the colonel for his distinguished service in the Civil War. And the second letter from General William Sherman, dated June of 1877, commends the colonel for, and I quote, 'his outstanding leadership on the western frontier against hostile Indians.' This colonel sitting here before you, an honor graduate of West Point, was, like all cadets at the academy, trained to fight Indians. Not only did he do so with grit and imagination, but the colonel's tactics and strategy used against the Indians are now the basis for the Army's new handbook on Indian warfare. This colonel is a military hero and should be treated as such by this court.

"If the prosecution has called all its witnesses, I would like at this time to call Mr. Carroll, the Indian interpreter, to the stand."

General Miles recognized some tension in the proceedings. In order to allow nerves to settle and tempers subside, Miles ordered a break. "We will reconvene in fifteen minutes."

TEN

March 1882

During the break Kindred sat off in a corner of the lounge outside the courtroom with his two lawyers.

"That Marlow is a lying, opinionated son of a bitch," he said to Captain Chapin. "You need to get him flustered. Maybe then he'll stop telling lies. Also I'd like to testify that I killed Running Bear in order to provoke a fight with the Ute, a thought I remember having had after I shot Running Bear. As you know, and the generals on this court know, provoking a fight with Indians has been a tactic commonly used by the Army for many years. Will the court accept that argument?"

Chapin responded, "No. If they do accept your argument, the generals will be acknowledging that the Army engages in such deceitful behavior. I've been in the Army long enough to understand that the Army would never admit to such a tactic. And they know the public's response to such deceit would be instant outrage—and a call for court-martials, and a demand that Congress reduce their congressional appropriations. You have to understand that the national press is here.

"Yes, the public wants the Indians out of the way and done away with," Chapin reminded Kindred, "but in a less violent manner. For the most part, the American public does not want to have blood on their hands. It's all right if thousands Indians die of white man's diseases, starve to death, or are killed in inter-tribal warfare. Such a fate is ordained by God, but it is not ordained that they be annihilated by Army bullets. That way the public can have it both ways. They can admit to living by Christian principles while allowing God to do their bidding. If you make the argument of a purposeful provocative action, you will find yourself, I'm certain, in the Fort Leavenworth prison for life, or worse—hanging from a rope. Stick with the self-defense argument. It'll carry the day."

Kindred had his doubts, but, still frustrated, he nevertheless followed the advice of his counsel.

Meanwhile, Marlow huddled at the opposite end of the lounge with Colonel Peters. "How we doing?"

"Just fine," the colonel assured him, "but let me lead your testimony if I bring you back on the stand. Don't say anything more than necessary in order to answer the question."

"I understand."

The court reconvened, and General Miles ordered Colonel Peters to bring forward Mr. Carroll.

"Mr. Carroll, you have heard the testimony of Mr. Marlow in this court, and you have, like others, submitted an affidavit to the investigating committee of General

Sheridan describing what you witnessed on the early morning of September 21, 1881."

"Yes, sir."

"In the testimony of Mr. Marlow, did he describe accurately what you witnessed that morning?"

"Yes, sir."

"Please tell the court what Colonel Kindred said to Running Bear when he was brought into the colonel's tent."

"He tell Running Bear that he have no permission to return to Uncompahgre Valley with corpse of mother, and that he disobeyed colonel's orders. He tell Running Bear she smelled up the colonel's tent and colonel wanted her buried immediately or put in a tree but she not going to Utah. Then he swear at Running Bear. I translated all of this to Running Bear except for the cuss words. I wanted to keep Running Bear calm so he not get mad. It no work. Running Bear shouted at colonel and called him the evil spirit in the Ute camp and then he jumped on colonel, take him to the dirt and strangled him. Corporal Marlow, Captain Olson, and I pulled Running Bear off colonel, who had pain and very, very mad."

Chapin asked the court if he could interrupt Peters's questioning. With Miles's permission, Chapin rose and asked Carroll, "How long did you study the Ute language before you were appointed a translator?"

"Sir, my mother a Ute and my father American. I learned both languages from mother and father. We talked both Ute and English in home. I served as interpreter at the Los Piños Agency for four years. When the Shavano band ready to go to Utah, Colonel Kindred tell me to serve also as his interpreter."

"Do you consider yourself totally fluent in both the Ute and English language?"

"Sometimes I have difficulty translating a word or phrase."

"Such as?"

"I have difficult time interpreting for colonel who want me to tell Indian chief he be a son of a bitch. I try to use milder phrase, like 'not a nice Indian.' And when it comes to translate the language of white lawyers, I think the word 'vicinity' means 'close by' or 'adjacent.'"

"That seems correct to me," Chapin responded.

"You need to tell that to Congress and Indian Commission in Washington."

"What do you mean by that statement?"

Carroll proceeded to relate to Chapin how Congress stretched the word 'vicinity' to include land over a hundred miles away.

Chapin could only respond by saying, "I'm sure Congress had its reasons."

Carroll wanted to say, "Yes, especially when it is to the advantage of whites and at the expense of Indians," but instead asked, "Can you explain them to me?"

"This is neither the time nor the place for an explanation," Chapin snapped back. Miles and the other generals looked annoyed at the exchange.

Chapin changed the focus back to Kindred's defense. "Maybe you didn't interpret Colonel Kindred's remarks accurately," he suggested. "You are, after all, a half-breed with Indian sympathies wanting to discredit an Army commander."

Peters objected to Chapin's remarks, not because he held any sympathy for Indians but because of Chapin's opinion and a lack of evidence.

General Miles agreed with Peters's objection.

After calling to the witness stand Captain Olson, who corroborated Marlow's and Carroll's testimonies, Peters said he'd like to call his next witness, Colonel Kindred.

The colonel moved to the stand with his slight limp and raised his gloved right hand to take his oath before proceeding to the witness chair. He sat upright with his polished campaign medals displayed on the left breast of his freshly pressed blue uniform.

"Colonel, please relate to the court the battles you engaged in during the Civil War and the Indian wars on the western frontier."

The colonel recited them from memory. He named the Civil War battles of Chancellorsville, Gettysburg, and Antietam and the Indian battles of Palo Duro Canyon and Slim Buttes, and then said, "I think that is a complete list, though I may have forgotten one or two," which he had—Petersburg, where he was severely injured.

Miles continued. "Colonel, did you not suffer a bad bullet wound to your right shoulder at the battle of Antietam but refuse to be evacuated so as to remain in command of your unit?"

"Yes, I was wounded at Antietam and later cited for bravery."

"And how many injuries did you suffer throughout your military career?"

"Seven," Kindred said as he removed his glove and held up his hand with the missing fingers.

"Now, please tell the court of your training as an Army officer, particularly as it relates to Indian warfare."

"From the very beginning of my military career at West Point, I learned of Indian attacks on innocent whites on the villages of New England and settlements in Virginia,

North Carolina, and Georgia, and attacks on wagon trains and isolated Army units in the West. Over the years I've witnessed horrible Indian atrocities. For example, I came across one abandoned Comanche camp where they left behind captured white women and children whose skulls had been crushed by a blunt instrument.

"Over the years I gained extensive experience in Indian warfare. Some years ago I developed for the Army the new tactics and necessary strategies now in use to confront and defeat Indian war parties in battle. Those tactics are now an integral part of the West Point curriculum.

"I heard constantly from senior commanders—in particular, Generals Sheridan and Sherman—from Congress, the press, and the pulpit that if this continent is to be settled and transformed into a fertile garden fit for Christian families, as commanded by God, such an outcome can only be attained with the containment of Indians on reservations. And if they refuse to move, we must eliminate them. In other words"—Kindred hesitated and looked directly at the jury of generals—"we've had to kill Indians to bring peace, prosperity, and civilization to the West.

"I faithfully followed the Army's strategy of eliminating the Indians. We allowed the Indians to starve to death after we killed off most of their buffalo. We sat back and watched with satisfaction as Indian tribes fought each other over shrinking hunting grounds. We also watched as God's hand devastated many tribes with smallpox. And once the Army had the Indians on reservations and controlled, they were dependent upon the Indian Bureau for rations and annuities. But at all costs the Indians must be removed from our growing nation. This was a very strong and consistent message from politicians, especially in the West, throughout my Army career. And it continues to be today, as General Miles, who sits on the court, can attest. I've acted on that message and, accordingly, I have been promoted through the officer ranks of the Army."

Chapin pointed out that the colonel suffered a broken leg in one Indian engagement and, similar to the bravery he exhibited in the Civil War, he remained on the battlefield until victory over the Apaches was achieved. The defense counsel then turned to the events surrounding the killing of Running Bear.

He asked, "Colonel, in your second encounter with Running Bear outside the tent, did you feel threatened by him?"

"Most definitely, particularly after he tried to choke me to death inside my tent. And when I *was* outside with Running Bear, he made a threatening move toward me. That's when I shot him. I did so in self-defense. In addition, I had every authority to kill Running Bear after he disobeyed my direct order stating that he was not to return to the Uncompahgre Valley with his mother's corpse."

"I have no more questions," Chapin declared.

Colonel Peters rose to cross-examine the colonel. "Sir, to follow up on your last response to Captain Chapin, how could Running Bear threaten you if he was on his knees, unarmed, with his hands tied behind his back?"

"It is always possible for an Indian to break or loosen the rawhide straps with which he is tied. I've seen that happen in my career. And if his hands had come free, Running Bear certainly would have tried to jump me once again to choke me."

"Even recognizing that you were armed?"

"Yes, he charged me in the tent in the presence of armed soldiers—Private Marlow and my aide, Captain Olson, both of whom were armed."

"And you also say, Colonel, that Running Bear disobeyed a direct order from you? Is it your habit to shoot and kill anyone who disobeys one of your orders without a trial?"

"If the person were a soldier, no, he would come before a hearing. Indians, however, have no such rights. They are savages, our uncivilized enemies, and must be treated as such."

"Sir, weren't you aware that the US government had signed a peace treaty with the Ute last year—a treaty that a majority of the Ute tribe agreed to, including the move to Utah? Also, Colonel, you must have understood your orders from General Sheridan. If not, wouldn't you have asked for a clarification? You were ordered to move and protect. Tell me, Colonel Kindred, how do you protect a band of Indians by killing their sub-chief?"

Kindred appeared ready for the question. "Colonel, you talk about peace and the peace treaty. Let me ask you, how peaceful was Running Bear when he tried to strangle me? Maybe you can explain to me why you or anyone else would try to protect an Indian who is attempting to kill you?"

"Could you not have taken Running Bear prisoner and brought him to trial after your return to your headquarters in the Uncompahgre Valley?"

"Captain, I did not make my military reputation taking prisoners."

"Colonel Kindred, were you aware that our Supreme Court declared some years ago that Indians are wards of our government and must be treated as such? That means our government is the guardian of Indians in the same way that parents are guardians of their children. As a guardian, you don't murder those you are bound to protect. Did you not have some moral qualms about killing Running Bear, who was unarmed?"

Kindred responded, "You need to remember we've been killing Indians in this country since the Pilgrims landed at Plymouth Rock. I took an oath to protect this country and to follow orders from my superior officers. That oath did not include the laws of civilian society. Indians are savages, and they don't have rights any more than wild coyotes or wolves have rights. As for moral considerations, I was trained at West Point, not at a Roman Catholic seminary. If there are moral considerations to account for, I've always assumed they'd be reflected in the orders from my superiors, if consideration is given at all. Not once in my entire military career did I ever receive orders from a superior officer with the mention of moral considerations. When ordered to engage the enemy and defeat him, I did so with all the means at my disposal."

Colonel Peters pressed for clarification. "Colonel, you seem to suggest that because you lacked a religious education, you therefore had no moral responsibility for the welfare of the Indians under your responsibility. Atheists make moral judgments outside of established religion all the time."

Kindred responded, "I have always believed that the moral considerations and judgments of our civilized society are not relevant or applicable when dealing with savages."

The defense counsel rose from his seat. "Also I would like to remind the prosecutor that this is a military proceeding in a military court. We are not in a civil court to decide how guardians must treat their children, nor are we here to debate moral considerations. The court and Colonel Kindred do not need to be lectured about unrelated decisions the Supreme Court made over half a century ago. I'd also remind the prosecuting officer that Indians are not citizens and therefore do not possess the legal protections of a citizen. Put yourself in the colonel's situation. He faced the threat of imminent personal danger, which clearly outweighed any of your moral considerations."

Addressing Peters, Miles said, "Colonel Peters, in your statements and questions you will be bound by military law and regulations."

"Yes, sir," Peters replied, clearly not pleased with the admonishment from the court's presiding officer. Then he continued his cross-examination of Kindred.

"Your orders from General Sheridan directed you and your troops to 'move and protect' Shavano's Ute band on their journey from the Uncompahgre Valley in Colorado to their new reservation in Utah. Correct?"

"Yes, and I'd like to add here that those orders also allowed me to use whatever force was necessary to accomplish the mission."

"How did you protect these Ute by killing one of their sub-chiefs?"

"As I mentioned, I had the authority to use whatever force was necessary."

"I understand that, Colonel. But what I don't understand is why you found it necessary to kill Running Bear, who was unarmed, to accomplish your mission."

"My authority as the commanding officer was being challenged by an Indian. I could not allow that to happen or I'd lose complete control and influence over the Indians and, in addition, lose the respect of my troops. I'd also remind the court that if Marlow had followed my orders and shot Running Bear instead of taking him prisoner, I wouldn't be here on trial."

"Colonel Kindred, we are dealing with facts here, not suppositions," Colonel Peters injected.

Peters continued. "Sir, I have to believe that your arbitrary punishment of Running Bear took the form of murder. Your personal insecurity is exceeded only by your lack of professional behavior. You acted more savage than the savages."

Chapin rose and shouted at the prosecutor, "This is a court of military law, not an arena for uninformed personal opinion! I ask the court to strike the statement from the official record."

"Request granted, and, Colonel Peters, you will refrain from any further personal opinions. Do you have any further questions of the witness?"

"Yes." Addressing Kindred, the prosecutor asked, "Do you believe you faithfully carried out the orders given to you by General Sheridan?"

"Yes, I do, in every respect. I believe I'm innocent of all charges. I would like to remind the court that the Ute forfeited any right of protection from the US government when they attacked and destroyed the agency at White River and killed its agent, Nathan Meeker."

Peters immediately replied, "Colonel, your statement is nothing more than personal opinion. You may think the Ute gave up 'any right of protection,' but your orders from your commanding officer were, and I repeat again, *to protect* them."

Kindred replied, "You talk about orders. What about Private Marlow? Had he remained in the Army, he is the one who should have been charged with disobeying an order. Specifically, my order to take no prisoners."

Marlow shifted uncomfortably on the stand as he recognized how Kindred now attempted to shift the blame and focus to him.

General Miles jumped in and quickly responded to Kindred.

"Marlow is a civilian now and no longer under the jurisdiction of the Army. Besides, he had legitimate reasons not to shoot Running Bear. Given the circumstances, it seems reasonable to me for Marlow to believe that maybe Running Bear had permission to leave the compound."

And then, looking away from Kindred, Miles addressed the courtroom. "Now, if there are no more witnesses from either side, I ask that you make your summary statements and keep them short. After that, the hearing officers will meet with me and we'll issue our judgment here tomorrow at nine thirty."

Both sides made their closing statements. The prosecutor focused on Colonel Kindred's failure to follow the orders of a superior officer in the unnecessary murder of a Ute sub-chief. He ended his summary by stating, "The colonel dishonors the uniform he wears and the country he serves."

The defense emphasized Kindred's commitment to duty, honor, and country throughout his long and distinguished Army career. Kindred practically puffed with defiant pride when he was described as a courageous officer who repeatedly put his life at risk serving this nation.

After the day's court session, Marlow, Carroll, and Colonel Peters shared dinner at a small café just off the grounds of Fort Leavenworth. Marlow asked Peters, "What did you think of Kindred's testimony?"

"What I don't understand about Kindred is that he was the product of the best education money could buy—private tutors and an Episcopal private school in New York City. He goes off to West Point and graduates first in his class. Whatever moral or ethical sensibilities he carried with him to the military academy, and he must have carried some standards after his schooling in New York, they appear to have been erased by the Army's science-laden curriculum and its total war imperative. I know from my own experience at the academy, only ten years ago, that Indians were portrayed, if mentioned at all, as non-humans, much like they are in civilian society. The cadets learned absolutely nothing about Indians, the various tribes, their locations, or their cultures. The few defenders of the Indians today are some of the liberal reformers in the Republican Party, sons and daughters of abolitionists who believe that Indians possess the human capacity to be reformed."

"Reformed how?" Marlow asked.

"According to newspaper articles, they want Indians to give up their savage ways as hunters and gatherers, and be trained as productive farmers. That's what agent Meeker tried to accomplish at the White River Ute Agency. Clearly, he failed in his unrelenting reform efforts. But the reform impulse continues to be strong in some areas of the East, particularly Boston, New York, and Philadelphia. As far as I know, none of these reform ideas, or the thought that Indians possess the mental capacity to improve themselves, have seeped into the military mind, and certainly not Kindred's."

"Can they be reformed?" Marlow responded.

"Of course they can. The question is: On whose terms? First we need to recognize that each tribal culture is different, with separate and distinct histories. There is a world of difference between the Ute and the Comanche.

As whites we recognize the difference between the English and the Germans. Why not with Indian tribes?"

"I'd hate like hell to have to work and reform the Comanche. It would be like trying to teach a grizzly bear some table manners."

Peters went on. "Reforms can't be made at the end of a gun barrel. The tribes themselves have to want whatever reforms are offered to them, not forced on them. I've been around long enough in the Army to see what works and what doesn't. The Ute are a peaceful tribe. But most of all they are pragmatic."

Carroll jumped into the conversation. "We no need to be reformed. Indians ask only that our culture be respected and US government keep its word. One Indian reformer come visit the Los Piños Agency on his way to look for new reservation site for us in Utah. Friendly man, but after he leave, nothing changed, except we ended up on inferior reservation site."

Peters broke the momentary silence. "We'll know tomorrow what the Army thinks of Kindred. My guess is they'll bring the hammer down on him to save their ass, and their appropriation, from that Connecticut senator who chairs the Military Appropriations Committee."

★   ★   ★

At nine thirty in the morning, the court reconvened. The courtroom was crowded with curious Army officers from Leavenworth and newspaper reporters who, among themselves, made wagers if Kindred would be found guilty, dishonorably discharged, lose his past service benefits, and be ordered to serve twenty years in a military stockade.

General Miles stood before his desk, looked at his notes, and announced:

"The court, after careful consideration of all testimony, finds Colonel Kindred guilty of disobeying a direct order issued to him by General William Sheridan. The court also recognizes Colonel Kindred's long and distinguished service in the United States Army. In light of this service, the court orders that the usual punishment for disobeying a direct order of this magnitude—imprisonment—is not appropriate in this particular case. The court orders: (1) that Colonel Kindred is dishonorably discharged from the US Army, and (2) that Colonel Kindred is no longer qualified to receive his Army pension."

A wide smile came across Marlow's face as he looked directly at Kindred, whose head dropped into his hands.

General Miles ordered the court adjourned. As Kindred passed Marlow, sitting at the end of the prosecuting team's table, he said in a harsh yet low voice, "You have not seen the last of me, Private."

A reporter asked Kindred if he felt he'd received a fair trial.

"I continue to believe, and so do most military officers who I know, that I had every right to kill Running Bear in my defense. The court has weakened the reputation of the Army and its mission to eliminate the Indians from this continent. I acted in self-defense. Throughout my long career in the Army, I have followed to the letter every order issued to me. I will, of course, appeal the court's decision."

Before another question could be addressed, the defense team hurried Kindred out of the court building and walked him to his small room at the bachelor's officer's quarters. He immediately began to question the competence of his defense team.

"How can the court accept the testimony of an ex-private over that of an active-duty colonel? The Army orders me to kill Indians. I kill Indians faster and more efficiently than any other senior officer on the western frontier. Then I'm found guilty of killing an Indian. What about General Nelson Miles, who sat on the court? He's killed hundreds of redskins up in Montana. What right does he have to sit in judgment of me?"

"Colonel, you're absolutely correct," Chapin said, "but we couldn't attack the head of the court."

"What a hypocrite!" Kindred ignored Chapin's attempts to mollify him. "My career is ruined. I've given my entire life to the Army. Now I'm without employment and pension. They treat me like a common criminal. Couldn't you have shown that those eastern liberal reformers, Indian lovers all, had undue influence over this court?"

"That would have been out of the bounds of our jurisdiction," Chapin responded.

"You can be sure politics were involved," Kindred continued. "Isn't it true the new president wants to placate the liberal wing of his party and that two-faced liar, Senator McCabe? All accomplished at my expense."

"I think you're right, Colonel. But we'll be appealing, I can assure you."

As he unbuttoned his blouse, Kindred cut off Chapin. "I'm going to take a shower, followed by a stiff whiskey. Good afternoon, gentlemen." He offered neither his hand nor any thanks for their efforts.

Outside the courtroom, Hiram Marlow was surrounded by the press. A reporter from the *New York*

Tribune asked, "The colonel believes he had every right to act in self-defense against Running Bear, and that the Army's reputation was injured by the trial. Do you agree?"

"The court has made its decision, and I agree with it. As for the Army's reputation, it's been around a long time, with many victories in its history. The court-martial of a colonel cannot change that."

Marlow walked to the temporary quarters assigned to him by Fort Leavenworth. There an official-looking envelope lay on his bed. He was pleased with the money order, which reimbursed him for a round-trip rail ticket to Denver, expenses to and from Ouray, and a three-dollar per diem payment. Carroll, who shared the room with Marlow, opened a similar envelope and, to his surprise, he too received reimbursement for his travel expenses and per diem pay. "Too bad we not slow down the trial and get more money," Carroll remarked.

"Maybe, but I'm sure happy with the outcome and thankful the entire trial is over. Honestly, I never thought those generals, especially General Miles the old Indian fighter, would find Kindred guilty. But they did save Kindred's bacon by not sending him off to the stockade, which he more than deserved."

"Glad I make the effort to get here," Carroll commented. "I want Kindred to suffer for all Indians he killed. Probably some of my relatives. I now go home with happy heart. Hiram, what you do from here?"

"Think I'll go visit my parents in Iowa, then return to my job in Ouray, assuming my parents are OK. You'll go back to Colorado?"

"Yes. Back to country near small town of Gunnison, where I grow up. It be hard trip back, same as coming here, because of snow. Hiram, you must come in the spring and look at my country. Good for cattle and open for home-steading with Ute now in Utah. The miners in area good customers. Pay all bills in hard currency or gold dust."

"I might want to give it a look come spring when I may have more money in my pocket. But right now I have to check up on my parents and my brother in Iowa."

ELEVEN

NEWTON, IOWA

March 1882

As Marlow rode the carriage into the circle that separated the farmhouse from the outbuildings, the place looked as if nothing had changed since his departure four years ago. Dead cornstalks poked out from the snowdrifts, which the wind had randomly distributed across the thirty-acre field. The rusted water pump stood at the same awkward angle outside the kitchen since the day Marlow, as a ten-year-old, had bumped it with a team and wagon, and the boiling vat, used to remove the hogs' hides, continued to give off the same sour odor as it did in his youth. Through the slats of the two corncribs, Marlow could see they were filled for the winter.

The blistered white paint stubbornly adhered to the house as it did to the hog barn and equipment shed. Outside the small horse barn, Marlow's father kept three wagons and the stone boat, used to transport rocks out of the fields, in perfect alignment. The farm's horsepower, two black Percheron geldings, looked out over the barn's Dutch door. He called to them. Tom, the smaller of the two, snapped his ears forward in response.

And, as always, hundreds of starlings patrolled the feed bunks for a stray corn kernel. Marlow remembered as a teenager how he'd sit for hours with his slingshot killing off the birds one at a time. His father demanded that Marlow bury the dead birds; he dug them a small cemetery out behind the horse barn. Today, the powder-blue sky was streaked with elongated clouds moving slowly to the east, the same sky that could turn into a dull haze and carry insufferable waves of summer heat or a blue-gray canopy of snow, sleet, and subzero temperatures blasting across the farm. Marlow walked to the kitchen door, where an unfamiliar black-and-white dog sat guard on the rotting porch.

The hug Marlow's mother gave her son reminded him of her physical strength. She could handle a plow from sunup to supper, outlast the hired help on most days during the corn harvest—shucking husks or shoveling the cobs into their cribs—and bake cherry pies at the Lutheran church in town that would cause two atheists to find religion.

Marlow's father, however, had aged physically. Calvin suffered his Civil War injuries—the loss of a lung and a severely mangled leg—without complaint. But the arthritis in his knees and hips had slowed him down and kept him inside most winter days, placing an extra work burden on Sam, Hiram's younger brother. Despite aging, his father showed no signs of mellowing in his seventh decade. Instead of requests, orders continued to come forth like blasts from a cannon.

He loved his two sons and wife but had a difficult time demonstrating affection. He did, however, smile upon seeing Marlow walk through the kitchen door.

"Hiram, what a wonderful surprise!" Then his critical nature took over.

"You look to me like you've worn down pretty thin. Tough winter or did the Army do that? Mother, fix Hiram some hot soup. He must be cold after such a long trip from Colorado."

Sam too was overjoyed by the surprise appearance of his older brother. "All the way from Colorado in this weather?"

"No, I came from Kansas by train." Then Marlow reviewed for his family his discharge from the Army, his work and injuries in the Columbine Mine, and his new job in Ouray, Colorado. He went on to explain, without getting into detail, the reason for his Kansas detour.

The family spent most of the afternoon sitting by the woodstove in the kitchen, asking Marlow questions and answering his questions about the farm, neighbors, and high school friends. The discussion of neighbors brought up the subject of Joel Swinger, the neighbor to the south, who had made an offer on the Marlow farm.

"It's a nice offer," Calvin said, looking at Hiram. "All cash for the land, the improvements, and some equipment. He'd bring in his own livestock. I always thought you boys would take over the farm. But I know Sam has thought about a different line of work, and you, Hiram, have never shown much interest in the farm. If you boys want to work the farm, I'll tell Swinger it's not for sale."

"If you sold it, Father, what would you and Mother do?" Marlow asked.

"With some of the money, we'd buy a small place in town so that Mother could be near the church and I'd be closer to the grange. I've become mighty involved in their politics—the fight with the railroads and their outrageous hauling rates for our corn from the town grain elevator to central markets farther east. Those bastards want to break the backs of those who feed them. A state leader in the new Populist Party in Kansas, Sarah Decker, told us at the grange two weeks ago we needed to raise less corn and more hell. And that's what I plan to do when I move to town. That's right. More hell and less corn. I'll like that!"

Newton never did impress Hiram. He always thought the town structures were only temporary until something better came along. But in his estimation, the "better" never arrived. The collection of wooden shacks, churches, and a rail station had remained the same as long as Hiram could remember. He recalled the small bank, where the owner squealed every time a dollar left the hand of the teller, his wife. The hardware store next door charged a good-size inheritance for a barrel of nails. And across Main Street, Mr. Birkenbaust, the druggist, could fix you up with some mysterious pills to relieve whatever pain ailed you. On the south edge of town, the livery stable sold swaybacked workhorses, the local engines of commerce, at outrageous prices. Scattered through town were four churches, which produced considerable noise on Sundays but few committed Christians. Along the rail track, down from the station, the grain elevator exchanged cash for corn at prices always too low for the farmers. And the grange hall served as the town's information center, where retired farmers swapped frivolous rumors, unconfirmed lies, and serious gossip. Newton's other news source, the newspaper from the neighboring county, carried a "Newton Column," listing who visited whom on Sunday, obituaries, and an occasional horse accident.

Marlow didn't want to appear to favor the sale of the farm for fear of disappointing his parents. Yet the sale could be his ticket to a new life of homesteading in Colorado, a thought he'd first envisioned when garrisoned at the Uncompahgre Cantonment. Maybe Sam would like to join him in the venture, he thought.

Sam spoke up. "Father, I know your arthritis is aggravated by long days in the field and in the feed pens. You and Mother deserve some relief from your daily chores, especially in the winter. Milking two dairy cows, slopping the hogs, chopping wood, and breaking ice in the water troughs wear a body down. With money from the sale you could live a comfortable life in town, and you can raise as much hell as Mother will allow you."

"He's had a plenty of practice right here for the last forty years," Anna Marlow added with a smile.

"Also I want you boys to know that if I sell the farm, the proceeds will be split three ways: a third to each of you and the remaining third to me and Mother," Calvin said. "The proceeds from the equipment and livestock will also be split three ways." The boys looked at their father as if he'd announced a week off from work.

"That's very generous, Father," Hiram responded.

"It is intended to be," Calvin answered and then announced, "I'm pleased to have your opinions. We'll put off any decision until dinnertime tomorrow."

Everyone nodded in agreement.

That evening Marlow and Sam talked quietly beneath the eves in their attic bedroom. "If I were Father, I'd jump at the offer," Sam said. "As for myself, I need to get out from Father's grip, away from the smell of hogs and the damn plow. I'd also like to see new faces—some big-breasted women with clean fingernails, who don't use pig shit for perfume."

"How about we partner up on a homestead in Colorado? I've got a good lead on an area where people say that cattle thrive, and it's close to markets."

"I just can't up and leave Father and Mother."

"But what if you stayed here 'til the place sold and helped the folks get settled in town? In the meantime, I want to return to my clerk's job in Colorado and stash away some more savings. In two or three months, I plan to file on a homestead in Colorado. I could pay a friend to file on an adjoining one hundred sixty acres that he'd transfer to you for a small fee when you came out in, say, late spring or summer?"

"A homestead, that sounds to me like more farming. I've plowed since I was twelve and that's long enough. I've thought of business, but you need some money to get started. I got no savings. Might try mining, but you don't make it sound very inviting."

"Sam, I'm not thinking of a farming homestead but one that raises cattle and maybe some sheep. We'd have to grow hay but, as you know, there's little planting or plowing with that crop. I understand that cattle and sheep pretty much take care of themselves if offered enough grass in the summer and hay in the winter."

"I sure wouldn't want to bet my future on sheep. What I hear about them woolies is that they wake up every day trying to figure out a new way how to die, and by dinner-time they're dead."

"OK, forget sheep then. Just cattle and some horses."

"Let me give it some thought," Sam said.

Throughout the next morning, Sam considered the Colorado homestead idea. Letters to his parents from his cousin, a miner in Colorado, talked about the natural riches of the state. Sam had read the promotional brochures of the Kansas Pacific Railroad, which made Colorado look like an automatic gold mine regardless of whether one became a miner, farmer, or rancher. *I really don't want to spend the rest of my life in Iowa,* Sam thought. *Look at Hiram and what he's done with his life. Certainly more exciting than harvesting corn, slopping pigs, and playing Chinese checkers with the neighbor's daughter.*

At dinner the subject of the farm sale came up. "Mother, what do you think?" the older Marlow asked his wife.

"If the boys are not excited about continuing to farm here, and that's what I gather, at least from Hiram, then I think we should help them start a new life. We can move to town and find a comfortable place. We're perfectly capable of taking care of ourselves, and we do have good friends in town, plus the church. I sure won't miss the winter winds out here, or helping with a sick hog at three in the morning when the temperature is below zero."

"Hiram, your thoughts?"

"I'd like to homestead in Colorado and raise cattle— very profitable, I hear—and in a cool summer climate. I've got some savings from my clerk's job in Colorado and, with my share of the farm sale, I'd be in good shape to start a small cattle herd."

"And you, Sam?" his father asked.

"Father, that's a very generous gift you would make to me if the farm sells. Yes, I would like to join Hiram in Colorado, but I do worry about you all in town."

"We'll be better off in town than freezin' our asses off out here in the winter and sweatin' to death over a plow in summer or pickin' corn in late summer. I just can't keep up anymore; my ticker is about wore out. I know that you boys don't much like the boredom of the farmwork. I can understand that. Also not many young girls around here. When I was your age, I also wanted to get off the farm. That's why I volunteered for the war. Besides, we can't afford a hired man. I think it's settled then. I'll contact Joel Swinger tomorrow afternoon. But I'm goin' to up the price to him, what with the new markets the railroad has brought us."

TWELVE

KANSAS CITY

April 1882

After the trial, Joseph Kindred took up residence in Kansas City, a city close to Fort Leavenworth, where he expected a new trial on appeal. In addition to the mental anguish of his court-martial, Kindred remembered how he'd sat through the proceedings in considerable discomfort. Before the trial, he'd visited a doctor in Kansas City recommended to him by the hotel concierge. Dressed in civilian clothes and using an alias, he complained to the elderly doctor of open sores around his genitals. After a thorough examination, the doctor informed Kindred, "You may have the clap or the French pox, as syphilis is sometimes referred to." The colonel had suspected he'd caught the disease well before he departed for the trial at Fort Leavenworth.

"Relate for me your recent sexual activity," the doctor asked.

"Normal sex with my wife, and on one occasion with a prostitute in Santa Fe." Kindred lied on both accounts. He had never married and spent over a month's salary on more than one whore.

"Was she Mexican?"

"She wasn't American."

"Mexican or Spanish?"

"Hell, I don't know. I didn't ask."

"How long ago?"

"About a year ago."

"What took you to Santa Fe?"

"Business. I'm a traveling salesman for a clothing manufacturer."

He thought back to his Army duty in New Mexico, where he'd given permission to the regimental sergeant major to bring prostitutes into Fort Union. In return for Kindred's acquiescence, the sergeant always ensured that his commanding officer was provided with some overnight company.

The genital sores began to appear about the time he transferred to Colorado, where they become more numerous. The irritation led him to scratch until he bled. When he picked at the scabs to relieve the pressure from the festering sores, the irritation only increased.

Kindred volunteered that he'd applied turpentine oil to the sores. With a look of amazement, the doctor asked, "Who in hell recommended that unusual treatment?"

"A vet I know said he'd used it successfully on horses with leg sores." Kindred was thinking back to the 4th Cavalry vet who swore by the oil as a common treatment for cavalry mounts and humans.

The doctor shook his head and responded, "Personally, I've never heard of the turpentine treatment. Some doctors say they've had very limited success with sarsaparilla root mixed with alcohol applied to the sores. You might give that a try. Also I'll give you some lobelia, a medicinal plant, to provoke vomiting and remove toxins from the body. I'll warn you, however, that neither of these treatments is guaranteed to rid your body of the infection. It may get progressively worse."

"When you say 'worse'—in what way?"

"More sores, body rashes, loss of hair, fevers and sore throat, muscle aches."

"I haven't lost any hair but I've had the other symptoms. Lost some weight, also."

"That's another symptom of an intermediate stage of syphilis. The advanced stage is particularly debilitating."

"Be specific, please," Kindred insisted.

"It can lead to irrational behavior, insanity, and eventual death."

"You reckon I'm in the second stage?"

"Probably, but there's no assurance."

"How long does it take to get to the third stage and possible death?"

"I've read of some men who've survived twenty years or more after discovering the infection. I want you to use the sarsaparilla solution I'll prepare for you. And the lobelia: take a pinch of the powder midmorning for four days. It is unpleasant, I know, but the vomiting might rid your body of the infection."

Kindred paid the doctor and thought about his future health.

★   ★   ★

After his court-martial, Kindred recognized the limited options he faced. No income, no benefits from the Army in which he'd spent his entire career, and no relief from his advancing syphilis. *What work am I suited for?* he asked himself. Only the Army could use Indian killers. He thought about hiring on as a captain with an emigrant company, which often sought retired Army officers to lead and guide wagon trains headed west on the Santa Fe Trail. The Kansas City newspaper often ran advertisements for such positions, but Kindred found none because, as the paper reported, Comanche raids had once again closed down the thoroughfare to the Southwest.

Kindred thought about returning to New York City, his birthplace, where he might contact old family friends who worked in finance, the province of his deceased father, as well as other family members. His uncle had headed the city's largest bank, the First National City Bank of New York, and another uncle ran a large brokerage house in the city and served on various corporate and philanthropic boards. In addition, his great-grandfather had served as Assistant Secretary of the Treasury under Alexander Hamilton. Two cousins ran investment companies that, ironically, raised money for the western railroad that Kindred, at one time, had protected against Indian attacks. Surely, the Kindred name and the social contacts that attached to the family, despite his father's discredited naval career, would be an entrée into the center of New York's social and financial circles.

In his youth, Kindred had thought he might like to follow his uncles into banking, but spending his life confined to a city office held no attraction for him. The most pleasant time he spent with his father was hunting in the Catskills. On one trip during his senior year at St. James'

Episcopal School in New York City, they visited the military academy at West Point. As soon as he viewed the uniformed cadets riding their horses on the grass parade ground, Kindred set his sights on the academy. His father, a former military man himself, encouraged his son, who had clearly demonstrated his love of the outdoor life on hunting and camping trips. Former Commodore Kindred arranged for the necessary congressional appointment.

Kindred hoped his mother might revive for him old family connections as he sought a suitable position in New York.

Dear Mother,

Recently the Army has had to retire some of its officers because of an excess of officers in the senior ranks— colonel and above. Many officers remained in the Army after the Civil War, and with the shrinkage of the Army by Congress, there are no slots where these officers can be placed. I am one of those who have had to take a forced retirement. I think this might be a good time to return home to New York and be close to you, if I can find an appropriate position, preferably in finance.

I should think that with almost a quarter century of Army experience, including my West Point time, and with my leadership skills, I would be superbly qualified for a senior position in a financial firm. As you can imagine, my problem is that I have lost contact with uncles and cousins and others who I knew in New York before I entered the military academy. I'm asking if you might make some inquiries on my behalf to determine what positions might be available. Currently I am staying in very comfortable rooms at the Empire Hotel, on Market Street in Kansas City.

I am in good health, except for an infection I contracted in the Army immediately before my retirement. I expect a fast and full recovery.

You could help me with a small loan of two hundred dollars until I start receiving my retirement income sometime next year.

I do miss New York and being close to you and the family. Please pass on my love to everyone and big hug to you, my dearest Mother.

Your loving son,
Joseph

Would the higher reaches of New York society have learned about his dishonorable discharge from the Army? He thought not. He knew that with his mother's social contacts, she'd locate something appropriate for a man of forty-five years and his station in life. As for the loan, she'd made one to him years ago so that he could buy uniforms immediately after his graduation from the military academy. Yes, he thought, the prospects of living and working in New York looked bright. Also the city would be the perfect place to find a suitable wife.

For all of the pleasant thoughts he projected for his future, Kindred still could not remove from his syphilis-infected brain his military trial and the testimony of private Marlow. *True, Marlow had related the events as they had occurred, but he lied when he said I ordered Running Bear to his knees before I shot him. That Indian bastard stood in front of me, ready to physically attack me just as he had inside the tent. Not only did Marlow's false testimony embarrass me, it led to my conviction and everything that followed.*

Marlow's testimony came to consume Kindred's thoughts. He'd fall asleep thinking about him, wake to statements of the prosecutor, or be interrupted, reading a newspaper, by the guilty verdict of General Miles—that hypocrite—and his court of underlings. A few drinks didn't help nor more drinks after that. *I know,* he said to himself, *a new life in New York will cleanse my memory and the poison in my body.*

THIRTEEN

OURAY, COLORADO

April 1882

From Iowa via Kansas City, Marlow arrived in Denver exhausted. He wanted to get to Ouray as fast as possible so as to get his job back and see Sarah. Snowdrifts had slowed the train in eastern Colorado for almost a full day while plows cleared the tracks. He tried to sleep but the unheated car and wooden seats, plus two crying babies, only added to his misery. Marlow ended up lending his buffalo coat and seat to the mother and her babies while he spent an uncomfortable night on the filthy floor with his blanket and bedroll.

He carried with him $250 in coin and notes folded into his boots, a small satchel for his clothing and personal items, and the Colt pistol he'd purchased in Iowa. In Denver he found a room and bath on Larimer Street, close to the rail station. The stationmaster told Marlow the train to Salida, the stop farthest west on the rail line but just short of the Continental Divide, would be delayed because of snow slides and a washed-out bridge.

While he waited two days for the train, Marlow strolled the streets of Denver. He had never seen city streets so full of human and animal traffic. Teamsters yelled at the work crews laying new rail lines for the streetcars. Carts, carriages, and wagons moved helter-skelter in all directions, obeying neither temporary signs nor angry policemen. Piles of lumber and bricks blocked passage on side streets and slowed traffic on the main thoroughfares. Massive block and tackles, which extended out into the dirt roads, lifted granite blocks to the higher reaches of new mercantile buildings. As best they could, pedestrians made their way along the boardwalks, all in disrepair from the horses that had trampled them. A multitude of unfamiliar languages surprised Marlow in the smoky restaurants with their inflated prices and watered-down whiskey.

In Salida, a small town constructed almost entirely of wood and a transportation hub for freight and passengers headed farther west, Marlow hoped to sign on as a teamster for a wagon headed over the Continental Divide toward the new towns of Gunnison or Montrose and eventually the San Juan mining district. Snows, he knew, would make it a long and arduous journey. On the Salida platform, Indians immediately surrounded the passengers, offering their services as guides for two dollars a day to the travelers, mostly prospective miners, headed for the San Juans.

At the Salida station, a wholesale merchant offered Marlow a teamster's job hauling a load of mining equipment to Gunnison. The merchant said he'd also hire an Indian guide to assist him. "Might be useful," the merchant mentioned, "especially in this snow where the road is hidden." The merchant added that he expected the wagon back in Salida in ten days.

"I was planning on a one-way trip to Gunnison and then on to Montrose and Ouray," Marlow responded. "I'll take half pay if that'll help." Surprised but also impressed by Marlow's offer, the merchant replied that he'd find a trustworthy Indian who could serve as a guide on the trip to Gunnison and then return the wagon and team back to Salida.

The merchant suggested to Marlow he should, for purposes of hunting and self-protection, trade his pistol for a rifle. Marlow found it easier to locate a working rifle in Salida than a good cup of coffee. Not surprisingly, the secondhand rifle offerings at the hardware store appeared to be all recent Army weapons. One was an Army carbine similar to the Springfield he shouldered in the cavalry. He asked the proprietor about the weapon.

"Indians bring 'em in here and sell 'em. They're either stolen or horse-traded. I don't much care how they get ahold of 'em, only that they're in good working condition. What you looking for?"

"A good hunting rifle," Marlow responded.

"I got a fine Sharps fifty-two caliber right here," the owner said, pointing to the bulky rifle. "I'd take sixty dollars for it. It'll knock down anything you'll find around here at three hundred yards."

"That'd be overkill for me and expensive besides. What about this here Army carbine?"

"That would be thirty-five dollars. It's in tip-top shape, like new. I'll throw in five cartridges."

"I'll take it, plus thirty more rounds and some oiled patches."

★   ★   ★

The ride to Gunnison through some deep drifts proved hard on the horses. From time to time, Marlow and the Indian would see elk pawing through the snow in search of some grass or see new bite marks on the aspen trunks. At the sound of the team and wagon, the elk would run off, though in some cases Marlow managed to get off an accurate flanking shot and bring the animal down within fifty yards. To vary their menu, Marlow hit a snowshoe rabbit at a dead run. In recognition of Marlow's hunting skills, the Indian guide flashed a big smile, opened his eyes wide, and nodded his head up and down for about fifteen seconds before running to fetch the red spot in the snow.

The two men worked as a well-coordinated team in camp and on the road through the deep snowdrifts. At night, they shared the same snow cave where they huddled close together for warmth.

Marlow guessed the Indian to be a Ute. They conversed by sign language—food, fire, camp, snow, shoot—the most important words. The word "Utah" caused the Indian to narrow his eyes, spit a stream of tobacco juice into the snow, and say "No good" in near-perfect English. He made it known by sign language that he'd come back from Utah during the last moon and would not return. Then the Indian picked up Marlow's loaded rifle, pointed it at a tree, and fired. Clearly Marlow understood his trail mate would kill any soldier forcing him to return to Utah.

Because of the deep snow, it took the men six days, two more than expected, to reach Gunnison. The town appeared prosperous, with boardwalks fronting new brick buildings, including two banks, numerous bars, two bakeries, a hardware store, and a law office adjacent to a real estate sales office. Horse and mule teams, heavily loaded and headed for the mines, crowded the town's main thoroughfare, alongside a small cattle herd guarded by a young boy walking beside the horned animals with a small whip and a whistle. A water wagon was making its delivery to a hotel at the major intersection for the road leading to the mining town of Crested Butte.

At the hardware store, they made their delivery and then headed for the livery stable to unhitch and feed the team. Marlow fixed himself a bed of straw and slept for ten hours. The next morning, the Indian harnessed the team in preparation for his return trip to Salida. Before they split, Marlow gave his travel partner a plug of tobacco. The Indian snapped off a bite and mixed it in his mouth with some hardtack. Marlow preferred his hardtack plain.

He asked the stable owner, Hank Perron, if he knew a half-breed by the name of Ben Carroll who lived in these parts.

"Sure do. He's a good customer, and he sure knows horses. I just bought a horse from him last week."

"He lives near here?"

"'Bout fifteen miles, out east near the old Indian agency on the Los Piños River. It's not that far, really, but right now in this snow you best be hitching a ride with an eagle or a giraffe."

"Is it a clearly marked road?"

"Yeah, when there's not three feet of snow. If I were you, I'd wait another month before trying to get out there."

"You got any horses for sale?" Marlow asked.

"You're not going to Los Piños, are you?"

"No, I'll wait a couple of months. Right now I want to get to Ouray as fast as possible." Marlow hoped his old job at the hardware store was still available. Also the prospect of seeing Sarah added to his impatience. Since the stage wasn't running because of the snow, he'd risk riding alone.

"Got anything that can carry me that far?"

"You'll be needing something with endurance." The stable owner showed him two good-looking stout geldings.

"What'll you take for the bay?" Marlow asked.

"I'd need fifty dollars just to break even."

"And what about that black gelding?"

"I need the same, but I'd sell you both for eighty-five."

"How about the mule over there in the corner? Ever been ridden?"

"He's as smooth and soft as a cloud. A bit splayfooted but he's safe and also shod. Thirty and he's yours."

Marlow frowned and said, "As a former cavalry trooper, I know my mules. The longer the ears, the better the mule. Hell, that mule's got the ears of a sow."

Marlow walked over to the mule. He checked his mouth for age, then his feet, and whacked the animal on the rump. The mule barely flinched. "His legs are a bit short. So are his teeth. I'll give you twenty and not a penny more."

There was a long silence as Perron contemplated the offer. "You know them mules ain't got the same teeth arrangement as a horse." And then after another long silence, the owner responded, "He's yours, and I'll even throw in a bucket of grain." The two shook hands.

"Where can I find a saddle and some panniers?" Marlow asked.

"Down Main to Fourth at the hardware store. They got new and used." Then the man looked toward his grain room and said, "I got a pair of panniers I'd sell for two fifty." Perron dragged two large, dirty canvas bags across the floor. Marlow gave them an inspection.

"Seen some miles on them," he commented, but then added, "You have another sale. Also I'll take a pair of those rawhide hobbles." He looked over the secondhand saddles, all too expensive, he thought. But when he recognized a McClellan, and selling at half the price of the other hand-made saddles, he bought it. To the surprised clerk he said, "If you've spent as much time as I have in a McClellan, you find them comfortable."

"You must be Cavalry?" the clerk asked.

"You bet. Six years crushin' my balls and rearrangin' my ass as a saddle pounder. Served some time with the 4th Cavalry at the Uncompahgre Cantonment."

"You the troops that took them Ute to Utah?"

"That was us. A long trip into some desolate country."

"You sure as hell must have left some behind 'cause there still a bunch of them around these parts," the clerk volunteered.

"They won't hurt you," Marlow responded. "But keep an eye on your horses, and trade for one of their fine ponies if you have a chance."

Delayed two more days by washed-out roads and snow slides in the rugged terrain outside Gunnison, Marlow celebrated his arrival in Ouray with two shots of whiskey at the Bucket of Blood. He took up the same inexpensive lodgings he'd left two months earlier. And after a warm bath, he settled up his account with the livery stable owner, who admitted Marlow's gelding had "lost a little weight through the winter." Marlow wanted to answer, "He'd be carrying more flesh if you'd have fed him better," but held off in appreciation of the two-month credit extension and the twenty-five dollars the owner paid Marlow for the McClellan, the tattered panniers, and the skinny mule he'd ridden over the mountains from Gunnison.

Marlow remained anxious about his job at the hardware store from the day he'd departed Colorado for the trial in Kansas. Mr. Platt made no promises the job would be available if and when he returned. Marlow walked into the store where Mr. Platt, clad in his usual dirty canvas apron with frayed pockets, sat at his customary spot behind the cash register. He looked up as the bell over the door signaled a customer.

"My word, what a happy sight to see you," Platt said, as he came out from behind the counter and flashed a wide smile. "Figured you probably stayed in Iowa and away from our winter."

"No, too much snow in Iowa. Thought I'd come back to Colorado and thaw out. Couldn't resist the temptation of returning to see you and Sarah and taking a dip in the town's hot springs pool."

"You'll be sharing it with a bunch of filthy Indians. They keep comin' back from Utah to hunt and use the hot springs. 'Bout the only thing that keeps them back in Utah is to collect their rations. They go back for their rations and then within a week they're back here. The Army is supposed to keep 'em on the reservation, but I hear the soldiers desert faster than the Indians escape." He stopped to examine Marlow. "You're looking fit, maybe a bit on the thin side—probably from all that traveling."

"I'm not a big fan of crossing the mountains in winter or spring. Tough going. I hired on as a teamster in Salida and brought a load of hardware into Gunnison over Marshall Pass. The worst part of the trip was after that, from Gunnison to Montrose and then here on a short-legged, splay-footed mule. Didn't see much game, and what I did see, I couldn't hit. Thought I'd have to eat the damned mule about halfway to Montrose. Would have been a small meal, however, mostly bone."

"Back here to work, I hope."

"I sure need a job."

"Yours is still available. Sarah wouldn't allow me to hire anyone else, hoping you'd return. On her day off at the courthouse, she'd keep the books current and often carried heavy loads from the wagons into the store. She'll be so happy to see you, I know. Come to the house for supper tonight, about seven—filet of mule."

Marlow laughed. "I'll be there," Marlow responded and then turned his thoughts to Sarah.

For the occasion, Marlow bought a new pair of jeans and a wool shirt. He oiled his Army boots to hide the ingrained grit, shaved off his short scruffy beard, and cut his hair to eliminate the knots.

Sarah looked more beautiful than he had remembered. Her auburn hair had been pulled back into a thick braid tied off with a red ribbon. Her face carried the color of autumn, with her full lips curved into a warm, inviting smile, echoed by the warmth of her aquamarine eyes. Marlow wanted to rush toward her and wrap her in an embrace. Mr. Platt's presence cooled his impulse.

"We're all so happy you returned to Ouray," Sarah said, offering her hand and then squeezing his. "Let's go into the parlor. I want to hear all about your trip to Kansas, the trial, and your visit with your family."

Marlow followed the scent of Sarah's perfume to a seat next to her and across from Mr. Platt.

"You look so thin, Hiram. Did they not feed you in Kansas and at home?"

"In Kansas I was at an Army post, so you can imagine the fare. At home in Iowa my mother stuffed me, but I lost all that stuffing on my trip from Salida to Gunnison and then here."

Marlow talked about the trial and his visit to Iowa with his parents. He avoided any mention of the possibility of homesteading with his brother for fear the topic might lead to more questions and an indication to Mr. Platt that Marlow was only looking for a temporary position at the store. Also any mention of a possible homesteading life might very well scare off Sarah and affect their relationship, which he hoped would flourish. For now he'd take one thing at a time. For that reason Marlow let it be known he was anxious to return to work at the hardware store.

"Both my back and I are so happy with your return," Sarah laughed.

Over a dinner of venison, Platt talked about his increased business with the opening of new mines. "We're fortunate here in Ouray." He went on to explain. "The government continues to purchase almost four million dollars of silver each month from all mines. And, as you know, we're loaded with silver here in the San Juans. New mines opening every month and miners coming in here from all over, including Europe."

In the Platts' small Victorian parlor with its heavy curtains and matching red velvet chairs and couch, Platt offered Marlow an after-dinner whiskey, which he accepted without hesitation.

Sarah switched the conversation to the trial. "What'll become of Colonel Kindred?"

"He's out of the Army and without any retirement benefits. Can't say I feel sorry for him. He's a bad egg, a mean, nasty character who deserved the guilty verdict. As someone said of him at the trial, 'He's more savage than the savages.'" Marlow directed the conversation away from the trial and its unpleasant memories to questions about Ouray and it new buildings, including a miners' hospital and school.

Marlow hadn't felt so relaxed in years. He shared company with a beautiful woman, had a responsible and well-paying job, and knew that his parents were being looked after by his brother. He'd given serious thought to homesteading but didn't feel so committed to that life that he'd cut off other options for his future.

FOURTEEN

OURAY AND GUNNISON, COLORADO
April 1882

Marlow worked long hours at the hardware store, relieving Sarah and her father of many of their responsibilities. Sarah was delighted to turn over her tedious bookkeeping duties to him, and her father had confidence that Marlow could maintain an up-to-date inventory. The work he found monotonous, but it paid well and kept him in the presence of Sarah.

In his free time, Marlow worked closely with his horse. The gelding had lost the energy and fitness of his Army years. Marlow rode him up and down the muddy mountain trails, and one Sunday rode him to the Columbine Mine for a heavy workout. He failed to see any of his former colleagues except for Big Jim, who recognized his former mucker immediately.

"What you doin' up here, Marlow? Lookin' for a job? We're hiring right now and payin' pretty good. I could use a good shift boss. What do ya say?"

"No, I like my digs in Ouray better than the bunkhouse, and the meat they serve in the town restaurants is red in color rather than gray."

"Sounds to me like you're spoiled. You all healed up after your accident?"

"Yeah, the Sisters took real good care of me. And thanks for sending on that check for back wages. Much appreciated. Right now I'm clerking in Platt's hardware store."

"My miners are always looking for an excuse to go there. I gather he's got a daughter who's a good looker."

"Sure better than anything I've seen around here," Marlow declared.

"We had some prostitutes up here a couple of weeks ago who might have given her some competition."

Marlow let it be known he wasn't pleased to have the subject of prostitutes come up in a conversation about Sarah.

"I wasn't making any comparison," Big Jim pleaded.

"You better not have been," Marlow fired back.

He'd seen enough of the Columbine from the inside to know he'd never step into another mine, regardless of the pay. For the time being, Marlow felt secure and happy in his job at the hardware store. Platt treated him well, almost like a son, he thought. The added attraction of Sarah, who often came to the store for a midday meal and helped him with the books on Saturdays, had completely transformed his life and expectations.

As spring gave way to summer, Marlow took long evening rides on his horse. On Sundays, he begged off church with Sarah to sleep late, but as the weather warmed, he invited her to join him on afternoon picnics in the flowering mountain meadows above town. She hiked like a trooper, Marlow noticed, and never feared to jump across a stream full with the late spring runoff. She brought the sandwiches and slices of pie, while Marlow brought the cider or hot coffee depending on the weather. They'd talk until chilled by the long shadows after the sun fell behind the surrounding mountains.

One day after a picnic, a letter addressed to Marlow from Carroll, postmarked March 1882 from Gunnison, arrived at the hardware store.

Dear Hiram,

When I go to Gunnison town last week, I stopped at livery stable. Owner Hank Perron say you pass through on way to Ouray and you buy mule and equipment. He say you asked about my location but he warned not to journey to my home in deep snow. Long, tough winter here. Much snow still on ground. You correct not to come. Indian cousin attempted the trip last January. We not find his body until the month the ponies shed their hair.

I remember we talked at Leavenworth about the land near where I make home. With local Ute in Utah, there is here much vacant land. The government surveyed last fall and it now open to homestead. I want to file on homestead site, but I not certain. Many problems to live around here for half-blood. Many whites think I no right to be here. "Go back to Utah," they scream at me. I say I a citizen, born to father US citizen. But to my enemies it my Ute blood they hate. They push me off the boardwalk in Gunnison. "Out of my way you savage," one man shouted at me.

Hiram, my friend, I want to stay here, I know my land. If well cared for, land make us a living. It is my home. I want you come here and give my country a good look. I know you like it. Maybe we homestead like partners. If you come, I take you to the best land where is good water and grass for cattle. I promise.

Messages from Utah say no one happy. My relatives lose sheep and many horses in move from the Uncompahgre. Utah country not what white government promise. Also the Mormons try to make trouble. I miss my mother, and little sister, also my aunts and cousins. But I want stay here and not go to Utah.

Please write and tell me your plan. I miss you and hope you come my way soon.

Your friend,
Ben

Marlow felt torn between his commitments to the Platt family, particularly Sarah, and his dream of owning a ranch and raising livestock. If it were to be homesteading, he'd have to wait for the sale of the Kansas farm and his share of the proceeds.

He didn't have to wait long. As if his thoughts were a call for money from Kansas, a telegram from his brother informed Marlow of a bank draft for $533 awaiting him at the First National Bank of Ouray, one block from the hardware store. An attached note indicated that another, smaller draft would be forthcoming in a week or so with money from the sale of the farm's livestock and equipment.

Marlow counted the bills and coins and placed the money in his old Army saddlebag. He assumed his parents were comfortably settled in Newton, enjoying a more relaxed life without the burdensome work on the farm. Besides, they'd be close to a doctor if needed. Yes, their move to town made sense.

Marlow made up an excuse to Mr. Platt that he had to return to Gunnison to pay off some debts. "I'll wait 'til the roads are dry, probably be gone about three weeks, and then back to the store. That OK with you, Mr. Platt?"

"Your absence will make it difficult for us, but we'll manage. Try not to make it longer than a month."

He walked over the courthouse to find Sarah at her desk. "Let me take you to dinner at the Bon Ton," Marlow invited.

"What's the big occasion?" Sarah asked.

"I'll tell you over a nice meal."

In a side booth at the basement restaurant, Marlow explained the sale of the family farm, and with his portion of the proceeds, the need to pay off some debts. "I told your father I'd be gone for about three weeks. What I didn't tell him, because I wanted to tell you first, is that I may be gone longer. While I'm over in the Gunnison country, I want to look at some ranch land, recently made available for homesteads now that the Ute have been removed to Utah." And then Marlow added, "Could be a good investment for the future."

He talked about his dream of owning a ranch of his own and the possibility that his brother might join him in a joint cattle venture. "Sarah, there may be an opportunity for me over in that country that I don't want to pass up. But at the same time, I have reservations about leaving you here in Ouray. I do, however, want to explore the ranching business. If I fail I will at least have tried it and learned from the experience. I should know within a year if my brother and I, along with an Indian friend from the Army, are successful. If we are, I promise to come back here and ask if you'll join me in my new life. Do I make sense?"

"You mean you may be gone from here a year? You must know I wish for your success, but Hiram, I shall so miss you, and the store will miss you. How will we cope?" She reached across the table, took his hand, squeezed it, and pressed it to her breast. He leaned over and kissed her on her cheek, wet with tears.

Sarah continued. "Yes, you need to try and fulfill a dream, but you must write from time to time." He leaned toward Sarah and before he kissed her again, he said, "I love you." More tears from Sarah. Once again Marlow felt conflicted by the choice of staying in Ouray with Sarah or ranching 120 miles distant from her smile. Maybe he wouldn't like the Gunnison country, but he doubted it.

★   ★   ★

Back on a familiar horse with a new pair of panniers, Marlow made good time over the rutted mountain roads to Gunnison. Farmers in the Uncompahgre Valley had started to prepare their fields for planting as they plowed over the teepee rings and fire holes. At the higher elevations, the aspens and oak brush had begun to show new life.

Once he reached Gunnison, he took a room at a boardinghouse. In the dining room that evening, he shared a table with a farmer who was returning to his home in Iowa after abandoning his homestead in Colorado.

Marlow started the conversation. "Tell me about homesteading. I'm thinking about filing on one somewhere in these parts."

"Well, sir, let me tell you something: Starting a homestead from scratch is real hard work, and it takes some money. You get yourself some land—that's the easy part. Then you need money for equipment, seed, building materials, a team, maybe some beef cattle or sheep, and some money for provisions. The newspapers and magazines make it sound so easy in a land of milk and honey. But I can tell you homesteading around here and even farther east can be pure hell in the heat of summer and the snows of winter."

The farmer stopped to see if his tablemate was paying attention. Then he continued. "'Bout the only folks who've made it around here are some miners, real estate traders, and a fair number of trappers. They're around the streams hunting beaver, bear, deer, and elk for their hides and wolves and coyotes for the bounty. I had a neighbor who'd made some pretty good money a few years back. But now the game is beginnin' to thin out. The grizzlies are 'bout gone, but no one misses them 'cept the trappers and a few Indians.

"Another thing 'bout homesteading that folks forget, and that's disease. Smallpox came in here 'bout five years ago and almost wiped out some towns. I heard Silverton had been hit real bad. Ain't too many doctors in these parts, and the ones that are here couldn't make it in the city. They say the doc in Montrose killed far more folks with his knife and his medicines than he saved. I know what I'm talkin' about. Lost my three-year-old son to a damned foot infection. Can you believe it? A damned foot infection, which the doctor supposedly treated, killed him.

And my wife, she's not ever been the same in the head after that. She's back in Iowa with her parents."

"You make any money for all your labor?" Marlow asked.

"I sure as hell didn't make money off the land. I only asked from my crops what I put in with my labor. Seems my labor always lost. I had a good grain crop one year, but the cost to get it to Denver ate up almost the entire profit. The only thing that made me money was the cream I sold in town. I tried raisin' beef cattle but I failed when two of my three steers died. The big grain and cattle outfits make some money, but they also carry some real high debt. Without credit, I couldn't get bigger. I found myself sucking hind tit. I never should have settled here. All the good homestead sites had been filed on or squatted on by the time I got here. The early bird got the worm. I got the rocks. I just got enough money to get me back to Iowa. Right now, I'm poorer than skimmed piss."

The conversation gave Marlow some second thoughts about homesteading. But at the same time, he had faith in Carroll's judgment about good land for livestock. He'd seen enough grain crops in Iowa not to want to duplicate them in high altitudes around Gunnison.

The next morning Marlow headed east to the Los Piños River, where, on the trail, a government surveyor directed him to Carroll's cabin. The primitive log structure squatted at the edge of an open meadow bounded by forest on three sides. Patches of snow remained on the north side of the ground shaded by spruce trees. From the edge of a log corral, three handsome horses nickered as Marlow approached. Out stepped Carroll, who ran to greet Marlow, put an armlock around him, and dragged him from his saddle.

"I hoping you come here. You get my letter? Too long a winter for this redskin. I look for a shortcut to hell to get warm."

"You don't want to be going there. You'd be mixing in with some bad company—folks like Custer and, probably in a couple of years, your buddy, Kindred."

Ben laughed. "I need warm weather. Also the wildlife. I see a bear yesterday starved to the size of a marmot. Come, we get coffee and brandy."

Inside the warm cabin, they brought each other up to date with their activities. Marlow, focusing on his life in Ouray, volunteered, "I was getting bored behind the counter of a hardware store. Selling shovels and bedpans isn't the most exciting line of work. Though I'll miss the owner's daughter. I'll see how our homesteading experiment works. If it doesn't, it's back to Ouray."

"A good looker?"

"Absolutely beautiful!"

"So why you here?"

"That letter of yours saying how good this country is, and that it's now open for homesteading. Remember, we've talked about ranching around here?"

"I remember. Tomorrow we go exploring. I have land already picked out. You like it, I know."

Marlow spent the rest of the afternoon adjusting the shoes on his horse and trying his luck at fishing on the Los Piños River, a short distance from Carroll's cabin. With a hook fashioned from a small nail, a plump worm, some silk line, and a willow branch, he hooked on to a rainbow but lost it in the stream's current. He managed to land two smaller rainbows, which he fried in bear grease to accompany Carroll's contribution to the evening meal.

"What in hell are these small cannon balls?" Marlow asked.

"My own recipe. I call them 'Bombshells,'" Carroll answered as if he were presenting a beautiful horse to his future ranching partner.

"And the ingredients?" Marlow asked after spitting out what looked like a piece of shrapnel onto his plate.

"*Ingreedents.* What that mean?"

"What's in the Bombshells?"

"Some chopped marmot meat, mixed with some water, along with onions, salt, pepper, and rolled into a small ball, then rolled in flour, and fried in bear fat. Very good taste."

"Thanks, but I think I'll stick with the fish," Marlow responded with a scowl.

The next morning the two men rode off to inspect the land selected by Carroll for their cattle operation. They rode through heavy timber up the drainage of an unnamed stream to its confluence with a smaller stream. They proceeded higher, through large, open grass-covered parks, interspersed by small groves of aspen and ponderosa pine.

"I've never seen such grass this early, almost belly high to our horses," Marlow volunteered.

"You can thank the Ute. They make the grass parks with fire. When I a young boy I set fire to this timber to make clearings for wild game and better hunting. We open up many parks, to east and west of us and also to south. The grass dry out in summer, but with some little water it come green again. It do not take much grass to keep my horses in excellent flesh. The same with cattle. I see many fat cattle come off this grass in September. Fat like pigs in grain bin."

Marlow stepped off his horse and pulled up a tuft of grass, inspected it, and said, "Deep roots." And then, like a chef inspecting his oven-fresh meal, Marlow added, "Dark soil with a healthy aroma—the best."

"Elk like it, more elk shit than wildflowers," Carroll volunteered. "Also I see many deer antlers and bear shit on our way up here."

"This country has been surveyed, right?" Marlow asked.

"I see surveyor last year at the time of the harvest moon. Tell me he finished in this country this spring. I think I see marker stone for section corner back a ways. People in town tell me this here land now open for settlement. We go to Land Office tomorrow if you want."

That evening Marlow and Carroll planned out their strategy.

"I'd like to file up here on a quarter section," Marlow said. "For my brother too. You could do the same. Seven or eight years ago, Congress allowed Indians to file on a homestead as long as they agreed to abandon their tribal membership. Except for a small filing fee, it's free. So, Ben, you could file on an adjoining hundred sixty. Then we three could partner up and run some cattle together. How about it?"

"But you say I must give up membership in my tribe?"

"That's what I found out when I did some research in the Fort Leavenworth library. Also you'd be giving up your monthly rations and annuities. But you'd gain a hundred sixty acres of land."

"I don't collect rations or annuities now, so I not giving up anything. But to give up membership in tribe for a hundred sixty acres. No. I am Ute like my mother, aunts, cousins, and many friends. Yes, I now live away from my tribe, a decision I make many moons ago. But I prefer to die in battle to save those whose blood I share than to give up sacred bonds to my tribe. Beside I have no money, little savings except those three horses," Carroll said, as he threw his head in the direction of the corral.

"We'll work it out some way," Hiram responded.

The next morning the two men rode into Gunnison and located the new two-room wooden shack that served as the General Land Office. A sign, "Homesteads Available," hung from the front porch railing. Inside, two middle-aged clerks stood by a table inspecting some maps. Other maps were pinned to the white plaster walls.

In the absence of a greeting, Marlow announced, "We're here to file on two homesteads."

Both clerks' attention immediately focused on Carroll.

"You Indian?" one of them asked.

"Does it make a difference?" Marlow answered for Carroll.

"Damned right it does. We're not lettin' Indians settle around here. A few years back we got rid of the redskins and sent them to Utah. Now they're coming back like a bad disease. They're not welcome around here. We're lookin' to be a region of hope—not a new home for Indians." Looking straight at Carroll, the clerk once again asked, "Are you Indian?"

"Part. My mother a Ute and live in these parts with my father, a US citizen, which make me citizen."

"I don't care if your father was General Grant, you got Indian blood. Indians ain't citizens. You'll get no special treatment here."

Marlow jumped in. "The man's father is a citizen, which makes my friend here a citizen. And besides, the Army considered him a citizen when they employed him as an interpreter at the Los Piños Agency. He's not asking for special treatment. All he wants is to file on a homestead, which Congress has allowed."

"So who are you, some kind of smart-ass lawyer telling us how to run this office?"

"No, just want to make sure my friend here is treated fairly."

"Your friend here, he's a Ute. Right?"

"He's half Ute."

"A member of the tribe?"

"Yes," Carroll answered emphatically.

"That's a problem right there. For an Indian, half-blood, or whatever, to be eligible for a homestead filing, he has to give up membership in his tribe and has to have been living in a 'civilized' manner prior to filing on a homestead."

Marlow spoke up. "I assume that working for the US Army is considered civilized living? If it is, my friend passes that test. Now let me ask *you* a question. What's more important? Being an American citizen or a member of a small Indian tribe?"

The clerk answered, "Being an American citizen, of course."

As Marlow reached into his pocket, he addressed both clerks: "Let's be sensible here." He placed a five-dollar gold piece in front of each clerk and said, "Why don't we just forget about signing the tribal disclaimer and get on with the necessary paperwork for this Army veteran."

The two clerks looked at each other, nodded slightly, looked at Carroll, and then at Marlow, who also nodded. "OK then, where do you want to file on this map?" the chief clerk asked.

Everyone's eyes turned to the frayed map. "Right here." Marlow pointed to a quarter section on the map.

"No, Hiram," Carroll interrupted. "Not there . . . here." The Indian placed his index finger on another nearby quarter section, one closer to Los Piños River.

"My God, an Indian who can read a map. Now where do you want to file?"

"Right where my friend pointed," Marlow replied.

"And the adjacent plot directly to north where creek starts," Carroll added.

Marlow was quick to notice that all the nearby quarter sections, except the one directly to the east of Marlow's, remained available for his brother.

"You're into some cold country up there. Better have some bear skins and horses with long legs."

"We'll manage."

"Just don't be bringin' in any more of your Indian friends. We've had enough trouble with them savages to last us a lifetime."

Before Carroll could respond to the last statement, Marlow interrupted, "Can we fill out the paperwork now?"

Looking at Carroll, the more disagreeable of the two clerks asked, "Can you write?"

"Yes. Is there a writing test involved?"

"He's written reports to the secretary of the interior, who is, I believe, your boss," Marlow interrupted.

"Look, mister, when I want your participation, I'll ask for it. In the meantime, just shut the fuck up. Understand?" Carroll had to physically restrain Marlow from grabbing the younger of the two clerks.

"I can sign my name, if that's what you are asking," Carroll volunteered.

"Good." The clerk then filled out the patent with the plot coordinates, asked Carroll for a spelling of his full name, dated the document, marked "NA" on the form where it asked for tribal affiliation and the disclaimer, signed it as the agent for the General Land Office, and then shoved it across the table.

"Sign here," the clerk snarled.

Carroll took the pen, dipped it in the inkwell, and signed at the bottom of the patent. For Marlow, the clerk repeated the process and, when completed, Marlow paid the small filing fee. The two clerks pocketed their gold pieces and gave a blank stare at the two new homesteaders.

"Remember, Indian boy, you have to make some improvements on your homestead within seven years, and it can't be a teepee." The clerk smiled at his weak joke and then continued. "Also you have to reside on the property. No lapses, no going off to Utah to see Momma Bear."

Marlow and Carroll walked out of the office through the waiting room and out onto the street.

"Real assholes," Marlow commented.

"I'd give anything if I could scalp both those sons of bitches and also get back your ten dollars."

"Don't be talkin' like an Indian. You're a citizen, remember?"

"Do all American citizens know how to bribe?"

"It's not a bribe; it's only a loan from you to me for our next poker game. Now we have to find someone who'll file on an adjoining homestead for my brother back in Iowa. I'll pay the man to stand in for him on the filing. I'd pay the person to do it in return for a 'sale of land contract' to my brother. Know anyone? And please not an Indian."

"Sure do. The owner of the livery stable, Hank Perron."

Within twenty-four hours, Marlow had arranged for Perron to file on the 160-acre parcel directly west of Marlow's and sign a document assigning the homestead to Marlow's brother in consideration for a two-dollar filing fee. The three-way partnership was beginning to take shape, at least on paper.

FIFTEEN

Kindred had remained in Kansas City ever since the conclusion of the court-martial. He wanted to be close to his doctor for treatment and to Fort Leavenworth in the event he might be granted a new trial on appeal.

He made his home in a cheap, transient hotel where his third-floor room faced the back alley reeking of garbage and raw sewage. A small collection of books sat atop a dresser with its two broken drawers. He used his Army trunk, blocked up with bricks, as a writing table. The closet hid his Army uniforms, two pistols, a buffalo-skin coat, some cotton shirts, trousers, a frayed Army sweater, and an India-rubber raincoat. He did not own a spare set of shoes, except for a too-small pair of Ute moccasins, a gift to him from Chief Shavano.

Kindred's plans for revenge against Marlow occupied more and more of his time as rejection letters arrived from

New York banks and insurance companies. A letter from his mother explained the negative responses.

My dearest Joseph,

Thank you for your recent letter.

I believe you misled me to understand you were forced to retire from the Army due to an excess of officers. Days before your letter arrived, a piece in Mr. Greeley's paper reported on your court-martial and your dishonorable discharge from the Army for disobeying orders from General Sheridan. If this is true, you have dishonored the family name by your horrible actions. The newspaper also reported that you had lost your pension. It is no wonder you need a loan.

I have given this loan matter much thought and have decided that, as you approach your forty-fifth birthday and for all the years you've served in the Army, you had to have saved some money. Most of my inheritance from your father now goes for my house rental. And my failing health continually demands payment to two doctors and a visiting nurse twice a week. Also I have my social obligations, which are becoming more and more burdensome each year. No, Joseph, you will have to care for yourself.

Word of your court-martial has spread to the highest reaches of New York society. Nevertheless, I made inquiries on your behalf with two banks and an investment house. You may hear from them soon. But do not get your hopes up. As your father learned in the Navy, a court-martial will follow you the rest of your life.

Regardless of recent events, I do love you and think of you often. Please take care of your health. Get yourself permanently settled, maybe here in New York, and please write again soon. It is your birthday next week. Please buy yourself a present with the enclosed two dollars.

Your devoted mother

A day later, a letter arrived from the president of the Bank of New York. "While you have extensive executive experience, your recent court-martial does not reflect well on your character or your effectiveness as a leader." Yes, Kindred thought, word of his court-martial had spread within the financial circles of New York. That son-of-a-bitch Marlow had, no doubt, informed the New York City papers.

Meanwhile, Kindred's behavior became increasingly irrational, brought on by his syphilis and exacerbated by a letter from the adjutant general's office in Washington informing him that his appeal for a new trial had been denied. The morning after receiving the letter, Kindred summoned the hotel day clerk to his room and ordered him to call for a mounted regimental formation for nine o'clock Saturday morning.

"Sir, this is not an Army post but a hotel. How can I do that?" the clerk asked.

The colonel yelled back, "You damned well know how to do it, Sergeant, *just do it!*"

His antics at a workingman's bar down the street from the hotel became so obnoxious that on two occasions he was asked to leave. When on a third visit Kindred challenged a patron to a pistol duel, the proprietor told him never to return to the bar or he'd be arrested. One Sunday, he rented a horse and galloped through the crowded city streets shouting, "Make way! Let the colonel through," all the while firing his ivory-handled pistol into the air. And once, while riding in the country, he challenged a stranger to a horse race for a five-dollar gold piece. When Kindred lost and refused to pay, he returned to his hotel with a badly cut lip and swollen eye.

He noticed the pus stains on his bed sheets and underwear had become larger, more frequent, and mixed with blood. He visited his doctor, who confirmed what Kindred suspected: his syphilis had worsened.

"I'm sorry to say," the doctor informed him, "but you've probably entered the third stage of the infection. I can see that you've lost considerable weight, and I notice a new ulcer on your neck. Any other ulcers?"

"Yes, a large one on my genitals."

"And your appetite?"

"Not very good. But that's because of that medicine you gave me. Sometimes it's hard to even look at food. No problem with drinking, however."

"What about your behavior? Is it normal?"

"No change as far as I can tell," Kindred replied.

"Have you been taking the medicine I suggested?"

"Yes, except I've eased off on the vomiting medicine. I've become weak from it; I had to stop. My bowels are so messed up that some days I can barely walk. Is there anything else you can recommend?"

"We could try another purgative in the form of a mercury compound. It, too, will cause vomiting and some bowel discomfort but hopefully with better results. Other than that, I'm out of suggestions. I will write a doctor friend in New York who has more experience in these matters."

Kindred agreed to try the mercury treatment. Then he asked if he could settle his bill for two dollars, the amount he received from his mother. The doctor agreed and added, "I do want to see you again in a month."

Kindred returned to his hotel, lay on his cot, and prayed that his doctor would find something to rid his body of syphilis or at least relieve the painful symptoms.

He thought about Marlow and his whereabouts. The ex-private's testimony had condemned Kindred. *That bastard lied when he said that Running Bear was kneeling when I shot him. He knew damned well the redskin was standing there in front of me and threatening me. And just minutes before he'd seen that same Indian try to kill me in my tent. I need to find Marlow.* Surely the Army at Fort Leavenworth would have an address for him.

★   ★   ★

Portraying himself as a relative of Private Hiram Marlow, Kindred managed to obtain Marlow's last known address from a clerk in the adjutant general's office at Fort Leavenworth. He knew that the easiest route to Ouray lay through Salida by way of the Denver and Rio Grande Western Railroad.

Kindred gave considerable attention to his appearance. How might he disguise his identity as he tracked Marlow? First he needed money beyond his meager savings. Should he take on the personality and dress of a lawyer, government official, New York banker, ambassador from England, or even a soldier? He liked best the idea of a government official. The Quartermaster Corps hired civilian inspectors to review and certify inventories of weapons, among other duties. Kindred felt certain he could pass himself off as a civilian inspector; he knew all current models of pistols, carbines, and, in the inventory process, he might help himself to some unaccounted-for equipment while inspecting various accounts at different posts. He created for himself a new identity. He cut his hair short and changed its color to match that of his new beard and trim mustache. A new suit, shirt, tie, and boots transformed Kindred into someone who appeared to be a person of respectability and responsibility. He opted for a hat as much for warmth as to cover his thinning hair, which Kindred believed to be a secondary target of his aggressive syphilis.

His finances consisted of $250 he had saved over the duration of his twenty-five-year Army career, barely an adequate sum, he thought, for someone without a job. He'd have saved more had the Army not required all officers to pay for their own expensive uniforms with gold braid and brass buttons. He thought himself meagerly compensated for his honorable service and felt betrayed by the loss of his pension. He knew retired generals who lived in affluent comfort in cities along the East Coast. Some generals had even gained property as gifts for their Civil War service from an appreciative city or state. Retired generals he knew occupied high executive positions in banks, insurance, and manufacturing companies. He had heard that General Miles, that bastard who headed his court-martial trial, received a generous stock gift from a railroad that his troops had protected during its construction. *What do I have to show for my service?* Kindred asked himself. *A frayed uniform, a pearl-handled pistol, an injured leg, three missing fingers, and a dismal future.* His payment for his new, self-appointed position as an inspector for the

Quartermaster Corps would be his compensation for past injustices.

Kindred made his way to Fort Riley, Kansas, and to the office of the regimental commander, Colonel Christian Gregory.

The plan was simple. Kindred would present himself as a civilian inspector sent from Washington to review and inspect their weapons inventory, and then match the actual inventory with the book inventory. Kindred knew from experience that actual inventories almost always exceeded the number of authorized weapons because of the sloppy records kept by regimental armorers. As the inspector, Kindred would take the unaccounted weapons with him back to Kansas City, where, he'd tell the Fort Riley authorities, they'd be shipped off to the nearest Army weapons depot.

"I'm Edward Barlow," Kindred said by way of introduction to the regimental commander, "and I'm here on orders from the inspector general in Washington to proceed with a weapons inventory and accounting of your unit, the 3rd Cavalry Regiment. I'd like to get started as soon as possible, Colonel, since I have two more posts to visit before the end of the month."

"May I see your orders, sir?"

"They were to be forwarded out from Washington last week. They've not arrived?"

"Not yet, sir."

"I'm certain they will arrive before I finish my work. It is the usual inventory we do every three years. I'm sure you've been through the quick, but necessary, process in past years."

"Oh yes, many times," the colonel responded in a tone of resignation. "I'll have the inventory books made available to you this afternoon. Shortly, I'll give the order for our troops, including officers, to turn in all weapons to the regimental armorer by noon tomorrow. I trust that will be satisfactory, Mr. Barlow?"

"Most certainly. I thank you for your quick coopera- tion. It makes my job so much easier."

"I can imagine," the colonel responded. "I'd invite you to our quarters for dinner but it would be beyond the call of duty to have you suffer dinner with my father-in-law. A total bore, but a rich one. He's involved in that new oil business they have back there in Ohio."

"I'm glad to hear he has one redeeming quality."

The next morning, Kindred went to the regimental armory for the weapons inventory where he joined the reg- imental armorer. The four Gatling guns on their wheeled carriages stood in a separate shed with three Hotchkiss mounted cannons. One of the Gatling guns had been dis- assembled to repair the firing mechanism. Kindred looked at the paper inventory and said, "Everything's accounted for here, Sergeant."

He then proceeded to the sabers; all the regiment's troopers and officers were authorized one saber and one pistol each. The saber count, including those under repair, came up fifteen short. The armorer explained, "Sir, we lose about one a month either in an infrequent battle or on training exercises. Troopers don't like to ride with them. They complain they're always in the way when reloading their carbines. Many just throw 'em away. Also I have six with bent blades which are being repaired."

"Sergeant, what about the pistol inventory?"

"We're over our authorized number by five, including the seven in our shop for wooden hand-grip replacements.

Our troopers like to use the pistols for hammering tent pegs. Not their intended use, as you know.

"As for carbines, we are ten short of our authorized number and the paper inventory. Again, I've included fifteen carbines in our shop under repair for bent barrels and broken stocks."

"Explain the bent barrels, Sergeant."

"Too many troopers use their carbine barrels as crow bars, usually to help a wagon out of the mud or to remove a large rock from a campsite. We had one jackass, a private, who bent the barrel, and then tried to straighten it. When he next fired the weapon, the barrel blew apart and took his hand with it. As for the broken stocks, they are usually the result of troopers using them as sledgehammers. Ten carbines I have accounted for as 'lost.' Too many of them, as you probably know, end up in gun shops or hardware stores in town."

"Sergeant, with the exception of your pistol inventory, where there is an overage, your records appear to be satisfactory. You need to submit a requisition for ten carbines. Also, given the problems you've had with lost sabers and bent blades, I'd suggest a request for at least fifteen more sabers. We've had many complaints from other units about the poor quality of the steel. The quartermaster general is looking for another contractor.

"Sergeant, please pack up the five surplus pistols so that I can return them to the Army weapons depot in Kansas City. I thank you for your cooperation during this inventory."

"Thank you, sir." Fearful of spending another evening at the Army post where his false identity might be exposed, Kindred returned by train to Kansas City with his satchel of five Colt .45-caliber pistols. He had hoped to get away with a few carbines, worth considerably more to a civilian gun shop, but the inventory would not allow it under Army regulations.

Kindred collected close to two hundred dollars in Kansas City from two small weapon shops, a hardware store, and a pawnshop. Pleased that he had some extra money, Kindred could now direct his full attention to the search for Marlow.

SIXTEEN

Gunnison County, Colorado

Summer 1882

The proceeds from the pistol sales relieved Kindred of the immediate financial pressures he felt after each doctor's visit. The last session provided no optimistic assessment, but neither did it suggest a worsening of his condition. Maybe the vomiting helped, he thought, but if he could only gain weight. His health issues, however, did not divert his constant thoughts from Marlow.

Marlow's last known address was a hardware store in Ouray, Colorado. Kindred knew the town from his time with the 4th Cavalry at the Uncompahgre Cantonment, a place he associated with bars, prostitutes, and foreign-speaking miners, and as a hideout for Army deserters. He must have disciplined at least seventy troopers over the span of his time at the cantonment. He did not look forward to what he knew would be an uncomfortable rail and stagecoach trip to Ouray or to the time he'd have to spend there.

Kindred rode in a third-class rail car from Kansas City to Denver, where he barked to a conductor, "I want this train to leave on time, or I'll put you up for a court-martial."

Minutes before leaving Union Station in Denver on the connecting train to Salina, Kindred once again addressed the conductor. "This train is a disgrace—filthy seats, dirty windows, and a floor that looks like the inside of a goddamned teepee. I expect you will attend to these matters here in Denver. If not, I'll see that you are demoted in rank." When the conductor disregarded Kindred, he shouted, "*Did you hear me?*"

"Yes, sir, I heard you. I'll have the matter attended to when we arrive in Salida."

"I want it done *now*. I am the chief inspector for this railroad and a retired US Army general."

"May I see your railroad pass, sir?"

"I don't have a pass but here's my ticket." Kindred's hands shook as he handed over his ticket. The conductor punched his ticket and moved on down the aisle, all the while shaking his head. Passengers turned in their seats and stared at Kindred.

At Salida, Kindred caught a stage to Gunnison where he connected with another stage to Montrose and Ouray. On both legs of the trip, Kindred, anxious about an Indian attack, rode the entire way staring out the window with his pearl-handled pistol in his lap. He constantly warned his two fellow passengers, "Be vigilant. There are hostile Indians in this area . . . Ute and Comanche, the worst."

Ouray had changed little since his last visit two years ago. Drunken miners spilled out from the bars throughout the day and evening. The police appeared less concerned with the rowdies on Main Street than the pack trains blocking the flow of horse and wagon traffic. Teamsters yelled, kicked, and whipped their mule teams while two policemen poked the animals with their nightsticks and shouted at the sweating teamsters. Kindred noticed the new sidewalks and thought the prostitutes were more evident on Main Street.

A sunny room at the new Eagle Hotel and a delicious meal at the Golden Nugget prepared Kindred for the next day's search for Marlow. That night, Kindred asked the hotel proprietor about Hiram Marlow. "He's a local, and last I heard he worked at Platt's Hardware."

"Not anymore. Left about a month ago, I believe. You'll have to inquire at Platt's. They may know his whereabouts."

The next morning Kindred dressed himself as a salesman with a coat and tie, polished boots, and a handkerchief in his breast pocket. A black derby covered his balding head, and he wore a pair of brown leather gloves to hide the missing fingers on his right hand as well as the ugly purple ulcer on his left hand. His mustache he darkened with a touch of shoe polish.

The "Platt's Hardware" sign covered the entire front of the brick building. Two small canvas awnings appeared more decorative than useful in a town surrounded on three sides by mountains that allowed only three hours of direct sunlight a day. The bell over the door rang as Kindred entered; Mr. Platt looked up from his bookwork at the counter.

"Good morning, sir. May I assist you?"

"I'm passing through Ouray and was told that I might find Hiram Marlow here. He's a former colleague of mine from the Army."

"Did you serve with him at the Uncompahgre Cantonment?"

"That's correct."

"And your name, sir?"

"Boynton, formerly Captain John Boynton, 4th Cavalry. I'm currently a traveling salesman for a gentlemen's shirt company out of Chicago."

"Hiram came to work for me after he testified at an Army court-martial in Kansas, where he gave evidence against his former commanding officer. Seemed eager to put all that behind him. He left here about a month ago. Said he needed to pay off some debts over in the Gunnison country."

"Any word from him since he left?"

"My daughter has received letters from him posted from Gunnison. No address other than 'general delivery.' Said he'd return in about a month, which is about now."

"You think he may be still in Gunnison?

"He could be. He talked some about filing on a homestead but I'm just not certain what his plans were when he left. I could damned sure use his help. A real good worker."

Kindred almost responded to the comment about the court-martial but managed to control his temper and asked, "You stock any forty-five-caliber shells for a pistol?"

"Sure do. For a Colt Peacemaker or the shorter forty-five-caliber cartridge for the Smith & Wesson Schofield?"

"The short cartridges for the Schofield. Twelve to a box, right?"

"Correct."

"I'll take two boxes. Also I could use some cleaning patches, rod and brush, and some lubricant."

"Length of the barrel, sir?"

"Four and a half, I think, but I'm not sure." Kindred pulled out the pistol from his pocket and handed it to Platt.

Platt stared at the nickel-plated weapon with the pearl handle. "Sir, that's a beautiful weapon. I've never seen the likes of it. Special model, right?"

"It's the Schofield—a Smith & Wesson model three. Gift to me from my battalion officers in the Civil War."

"It's a beauty. You sure don't want to lose that one." Platt put the order together for Kindred. As he made change for Kindred's ten-dollar gold piece, Platt said, "Sir, take care of yourself and that Schofield."

"I hear the road is safe between here and Gunnison?"

"Now that the Indians have mostly moved out, yes, it's a lot safer. Of course there are a few trail thieves, just like anywhere else. Also you'll see an occasional Indian who's returned from Utah either to hunt or take a job. They are supposed to stay on their new reservation but some won't, and the Army is so undermanned they're incapable of keeping 'em on the reservation."

On the way out the door, Kindred turned to Platt and said, "Thanks. I'll keep an eye out for thieves and Indians."

On the stage to Gunnison, Kindred shared a padded bench with a farmer on his way back home to Kansas. He inquired about Kindred's line of work.

"Traveling salesman. Men's dress shirts. Travel all over Colorado and Kansas for a Chicago manufacturer." Kindred did not offer his name or an alias.

The farmer asked about rail connections in and out of Denver, and, from Kindred's vague and in some cases uninformed answers, he wasn't so sure about Kindred's profession. His doubts were confirmed by the sight of a pearl-handled pistol protruding from Kindred's left trouser pocket.

"I see you're carrying a pistol. Expecting trouble along the way?"

"The last time I traveled this route, I had to shoot three Indians to clear the path for the stage. Can't be too careful in this part of the country. You never know about the redskins. Best carry a weapon. Headed for Kansas, are you?"

"Yep, goin' back to see my family. You got a family?"

"Never had the urge to marry. Maybe someday."

The rough road combined with the hard-sprung stage irritated Kindred's ulcers. He could feel where the pus had leaked through the gauze dressings into his underwear. He shouted to the driver to stop so he could "relieve" himself. Behind a grove of oak brush, Kindred removed the bloody dressings, tried to squeeze the ulcers dry of bloody pus, and applied some alcohol from his flask before covering the swollen ulcers with clean gauze. Immediately to his front about thirty yards away, Kindred thought he saw three or four turkey feathers moving behind the brush. *Ute*, he figured, given their use of wild turkey feathers. *They, and their Indian allies, will follow me to my death.*

He knelt down, pulled the loaded pistol from his pants pocket, and cocked the trigger. He listened for movement in the brush and a glimpse of his pursuer. Nothing. Holding the pistol in his left hand and steadying it with his gloved right hand, Kindred aimed the weapon at the middle of the small clump of oak brush, and fired. All quiet except for the sound of the bullet as it ricocheted off a rock in the background. Satisfied that no Ute had stalked him, Kindred returned to coach.

"Did I hear a pistol shot?" the driver asked.

"Yep, I took care of a Ute, who probably wanted to rob us. His robbing days are over."

The Kansan leaned out the coach window. "Any more of them?"

"If he had any company, I'm certain I scared them off," Kindred responded with considerable bravado. "Let's get going, Sergeant," Kindred yelled at the driver.

Kindred wanted to keep the conversation away from himself and his background. He asked his traveling companion about his line of work.

"Started out here in the grocery business. It's what I did in Kansas. My credit dried up and that was it."

"No banks around you could rob?" Kindred asked.

The passenger thought Kindred was making a joke, but his serious frown and presence of a pistol suggested otherwise. "That's not really my line of work. Do you use that pistol you're carrying for such work?"

"Been known to on occasion."

"So you're not really a traveling salesman, is that it?"

"I'm a salesman now, but in my youth I sure raised hell."

All of a sudden the stage hit a deep hole. The two passengers bounced off their seats before Kindred shouted at the driver, "Sergeant, watch where in hell you're going! You 'bout broke our backs in here. If you can't do better than that, I'll have you relieved of duty!" Marlow turned back to his companion, successfully containing his emotions under a false veneer of gentility. "Sorry for the interruption. Continue your story, sir."

The farmer thought it strange that the salesman referred to the driver as sergeant, but he thought it best to continue the topic of the conversation rather than ask questions. "Over the years I harvested more rocks than oats. I'd have switched over to cattle—good grass country— but it takes some savings and credit, neither of which I had. So here I am, headed back home, a failure, I guess. But from what I hear and see around these parts, a lot of folks, like me, never did find the elephant. You only hear about the few who made it, and they were well financed before they arrived here. Not a word about those who didn't make it. No one wants to read about death, disease, bankruptcy, and depression, except maybe those folks who make money off of someone else's misfortune."

"Like land companies," Kindred added.

"You got that right. Ain't too many of the original homesteaders still around. Like me, they sold what they could and moved on. Rather than pissing my money away trying to homestead, I'd have been better off if I'd played craps." He took a breath and continued in an angry tone "Hell, I know of two homesteaders up on a mesa near the small town of Dallas who just walked away, left everything behind. A squatter is on one of those places now. And prairie dogs run the other one."

"Bad luck, I'd say . . . maybe just lazy like many home-steaders I hear about."

"Not a lazy bone in their bodies, just bad land," the Kansan countered.

The two men dozed off as the coach crossed over El Cielo Pass before dropping down into the Gunnison valley.

Kindred located himself a comfortable room in a boardinghouse close to the livery stable, but only after a long and nasty argument with the proprietor about the daily rate.

"For that price I should be served breakfast in bed," Kindred argued.

"If you don't like our rates, I'd suggest you go down the road to another establishment that your pocketbook can afford."

"I expect clean sheets and fresh air."

"They're included."

"Do you take credit?"

"Cash only."

"What? I've never heard of such a thing. I've always been granted credit wherever I travel."

"Try the hotel down on the corner. Maybe they'll give you credit, but their rates are higher."

"Never seen the likes of it. OK, give me that pen."

He signed the registry as "Christian Fletcher," occupation "Capitalist," the common description of visiting mine investors who frequented western Colorado.

Kindred climbed the stairs to his small room facing the street and furnished with a single bed and a horsehair mattress, a writing desk, bedside table, and oil lamp. In the shared bathroom down the hall, he changed his dressings. A new small ulcer had appeared on his waist just below the belt line.

In his room, he noticed that over the desk hung a framed colored print of a cavalry officer on horseback pointing his sword toward a band of retreating Indians. His thoughts turned to his fighting days with the Comanche. He had whipped them in their own country, had taken some scalps, weapons, and ponies. One Indian translator told Kindred that the Indians feared him more than any other soldier. They said Bad Hand could read their mind; he knew exactly where they hid and what terrain provided them the greatest advantages for an ambush. With Bad Hand in the country, the Comanche admitted they'd have a difficult time recovering their homeland, but recover it they would.

For all of my victories and kudos, what in hell am I doing here? Kindred asked himself. *Sitting in a fleabag hotel in a desolate mountain town and chasing an ex–Army private whose only claim to fame is his ability to lie before a panel of generals who were dumb enough to believe him. The country needs men like me to protect it from those bloodthirsty redskins.*

He lay on his bed thinking about his court-martial and Marlow. *When I find him, and I will, how shall I kill him? Pistol, rifle, or saber? I know damned well I'll scalp him, and, like the Comanche, cut off his balls and stick the little oysters in his mouth. Whoever finds him will think that an Indian killed him. But first I must find him, reconnoiter the situation, and make my plan.*

SEVENTEEN

MARLOW HOMESTEAD

Summer 1882

Marlow and Carroll wasted little time moving onto their
adjacent homestead properties that, from the beginning,
they operated as one ranch. In Gunnison, they purchased
a Morgan work team and a heavy-duty wagon, chains,
saws, axes, cedar shingles, milled planks and boards, nails,
and a variety of hand tools. Within six weeks, they'd built
a three-room cabin chinked with clay mixed with muslin and dead grass, a stone fireplace, and a rough planked
floor covered with two bear skins that Carroll brought
to the partnership. With his axe skills, Carroll could flat-
ten the top and bottom surfaces of a log to fit flush with
the other spruce timbers. The two men notched the corner logs to add strength and stability to the structure. A
secondhand wood stove, a cast-iron sink, and a wooden
worktable faced the north wall; another handcrafted table
and two spruce stumps occupied the center of the main

room. One bedroom, which the two men shared, lay off to the east, while a second bedroom, for Marlow's brother but temporarily used for storage, occupied the west side of the cabin. Two plank doors, front and rear, with leather hinges, allowed for air circulation in the midsummer heat. Marlow thought the finished cabin comfortable and, he hoped, attractive enough for Sarah should they marry.

The cabin, partially shaded by a grove of aspens, was supplied by a gallon-a-minute spring that surfaced from a mossy rock formation thirty yards away. A shallow trench carried the water to a half-buried wooden barrel outside the back door. A folded muslin sheet filtered out leaves, dirt, and small rodents. Two large, south-facing grass fields, separated by a stand of giant spruce trees, were within walking distance of the cabin. The partners planned to build, before the winter season, two additional structures close to the cabin—an equipment shed and a lean-to. A barn for hay storage and winter protection for the horses would have to wait another few months. They called their ranch the Diamond J, after they bought the brand from a departing homesteader.

The two men figured that they'd use one of the open fields, of about thirty acres, for summer grazing and the second, larger field for hay production and winter feed for the team, two saddle horses, and whatever cattle they could immediately afford. The field would need to be plowed, harrowed, and cleared of rocks before seeding. They hoped for a good grass crop by next summer—a mixture of timothy, brome, and a small amount of red clover. In the meantime they'd have to budget for the purchase of hay their first winter.

With the assistance of financing from the hardware store in Gunnison, Marlow signed for the purchase of a harrow, a seed drill, a single-bladed sulky plow, and five rolls of Glidden's barbed wire. The remaining cash from his portion of the family's farm sale went toward the purchase of a three-year-old Jersey milk cow, four middle-aged Hereford cows with calves, and a cranky but well-muscled gelding saddle horse.

They soon met their neighbor, Franz Keller, a German homesteader who'd just settled adjacent to the Marlow-Carroll ranch. Keller, his wife, and his two young sons had moved from Illinois with a small herd of cattle and a wagonload of household furnishings. At their first meeting, Keller pointed out to Marlow and Carroll the exact location of their common property line and his expectation that the Diamond J cattle would not wander onto his pastures. Marlow reminded the newcomer that Colorado's new fence laws required a land owner to "fence out" neighboring livestock.

"I'll do the same," Marlow volunteered, "and where we have a common fence, I expect to share the cost in materials and labor with you, Mr. Keller." The German failed to acknowledge the suggestion.

Building an irrigation ditch and fencing became the first order of business for both ranches. Marlow plowed a ditch off of Los Piños that led to the head of the Diamond J and above the two meadows. Keller helped build the head gate and divider box where the two ranches split evenly their appropriated water from Los Piños.

For over a week after Keller moved in, Marlow and Carroll cut posts, dug postholes, cleared brush for the fence line, and stretched the Glidden wire. Within ten days, they'd completed their half of the shared fence line. Keller was slow to start and even slower to finish. His half of the fence consisted of long piles of dead tree limbs, some boards, and patches of smooth wire single-strung between trees. Not surprising to Marlow, the makeshift fence failed to keep the Diamond J livestock out of Keller's property or keep Keller's cattle on his place. The situation, plus a property line dispute, came to a head one day when Keller appeared on horseback at Marlow's work shed. Behind him, he dragged a calf with a rope.

"Dis dead calf, it's yours. I just shot it," Keller said casually, as if announcing the time of day. The head wound was still leaking blood, and the calf's eyes had rolled back to where their color matched the overcast sky.

Carroll pulled a pistol from his holster.

"I should put a bullet in your fat belly," Carroll said, as he cocked the hammer on his pistol. "Why in hell you kill calf?"

Marlow jumped in. "Ben, just calm down before someone gets hurt." Addressing Keller, Marlow said, "I suppose you killed the calf because he stepped on your property?"

"Dat's correct. And I do the same again if I see utter animals on my land."

"Listen up, Keller. You know the law. You fence to keep animals out and share the expense on a common fence line. We've built our half, and it's animal tight. That thing you built is nothing more than a long, thin line of brush, mixed with a lot of air, and a couple of pieces of wire thrown in. I'd suggest you build a proper fence or we'll get the sheriff out here and have you arrested. How'd you kill 'em?"

"Vit dis pistol," Keller said as he pulled a Colt .45 Peacemaker from his overalls pocket.

"Don't point that thing at me, or I put you to the ground," Carroll said with considerable irritation as he snapped back the trigger on the rifle in his right hand.

Keller repositioned his weapon and then asked, "You Indian? I taught all Indians moved out of here. Dat's vy ve come to dis area to homestead."

"Not so. There be a bunch of us wild ones still here, like me, and I tell you right now we no like Germans."

"Ve try and verk mit our neighbors," Keller responded.

"You need to try real hard." And then Carroll shouted, "*In the meantime, fix your fence!*"

Not taking his eyes off Carroll, Keller dismounted, took the rope off the dead calf's neck, remounted, and rode off, coiling the rope as his small swayback mare moved into a slow lope.

"That son of a bitch shows up here again with a calf, he'll get a belly full of lead," Marlow said, adding a healthy spit for emphasis. "Best we keep an eye on that German."

Two days later, another argument erupted between Keller and Marlow when Marlow noticed someone had closed off the Diamond J's share of the ditch water at the divider box. He reopened Diamond J's side of the box, which reduced the flow into Keller's ditch. Knowing that Keller set his water early in the morning, Marlow went to the divider box at six thirty a.m. the next morning and hid in the brush. Within a half hour Keller showed up with his shovel. He closed off the Diamond J water and went to resetting his water, now double the volume. Marlow stepped out of the brush, pulled his pistol, and said, "You do that one more time and you'll be floating dead down Los Piños. Now remove the board from my side of the box!"

Keller did as he was ordered, and, as he walked away from the box, said, "No reason to git mad over a little vater."

"You damned well better learn how valuable water is in this country. If I catch you taking any more of my water, I'll put some lead into that sausage belly of yours." Marlow fired a round into the air for emphasis. Keller jumped at the noise and then ran toward his cabin.

That evening, to calm his nerves and take his mind away from Keller, Marlow wrote to Sarah.

My Dear Sarah,

I hope you received my last short letter saying I arrived safely in Gunnison about a month ago. Carroll, my Indian friend, and I have filed on adjoining homesteads. We have made great progress building a cabin, developing a spring, and clearing some land. It is too late to plant but we will be ready to seed come May. Our livestock, a couple of cows with calves, are thriving on the wonderful grass we have. I can also brag that I've purchased some equipment and a fine team of black Morgans. My saddle horse, however, I won't brag on.

How is everything at the store? When I go into Gunnison town I get some news about Ouray and how well the mines are doing, but no letter from you. I miss hearing from you. Please write soon.

To be very honest with you, I do like my new life here ranching. I much prefer to work outside with animals and in the fields rather than inside. It must be my farming background. I do want to stay here but I'm very lonely without you. I want very much to marry you and make my life with you here on the homestead. I wish I could come to Ouray this week and make this proposal in person, but I have a problem here with a neighbor that I should have solved within a month. Then I want to come to Ouray and ask your father for your hand. You need to put him in the right mood so that he'll say yes to our marriage and your move here to the ranch. Please let me know if you think he'll agree or disagree.

I must close now and prepare supper. I'm usually the cook on this outfit.

My darling, Sarah, how I love and miss you. If the envelope were big enough, I'd enclose a big hug and a kiss.

With all my love,
Hiram

★   ★   ★

While Marlow tended to his ranch, including giving lessons to his neighbor about the importance of water, Kindred, not far away, sat on his bed in his Gunnison hotel room contemplating his next move. He walked to the livery stable in search of a saddle horse. By midsummer the stable's inventory had diminished. The owner, Hank Perron, showed off some aged, swayback geldings; a good-looking but fine-boned small mare; two wild-eyed, thin Indian ponies; and a big, muscular bay stallion. Kindred nodded his head toward the stallion, knowing there had to be something wrong with the horse or he'd have sold long ago. He asked, "What's his problem?"

"Got a wire cut on that right hind leg, some tendon damage, but not bad. It forces his hoof out at a bit of an angle. I've shod him special with a small pad on the outside of his foot, which helps even the weight on his shinbone. He's adjusted to it well. Ride him; you'll see. Big, powerful thing. He'll go all day and never give you trouble. Been an Army stallion. See the brand?"

Kindred looked him over carefully. Good hard feet, well-muscled, the teeth suggested nine or ten years, although Perron said seven. Perron put a halter with a long lead rope on the horse, took him out to the small circular corral behind the stalls, and had the stallion trot in a circle.

"Don't see no problem with that leg, do ya?" Perron said.

"Circle him around the other way," Kindred commanded.

Perron and the horse reversed direction.

"See, still no problem. He'll give you an honest day's work every time you saddle him. You want to ride 'em?"

Kindred nodded, and the proprietor threw a saddle up on the stallion's big back. "He'll ride with that halter. No need for a rein and bit."

Kindred took the halter, adjusted the stirrups, limped over to a mounting stump designed for kids and women, and pulled himself into the too-small saddle with his gloved hand. He trotted around the ring, pulled the horse to a quick stop, backed him up, and then eased him into a slow, soft canter before leading him up to the proprietor. Kindred slid off the saddle gently, holding the halter rope. "You can tell he's been Army trained. I'll take him for twenty-five dollars. Got any McClellans for sale?"

"I've been asking fifty for that stallion but I'm anxious to get rid of him after boarding him for two months. As for a McClellan, I didn't know that anyone rode those saddles voluntarily. My brother says after he was in the cavalry for a couple of years, his balls grew to the size and color of watermelons. Says they're still that size, different color though."

"They can be uncomfortable 'til you get used to them. I've spent a few years in them so I like 'em."

"Cavalry?"

"Yeah, Civil War."

Perron dragged out three well-used McClellans.

"I'll take that one, plus that cavalry bit and a new set of braided reins. I'll be boarding him here for no longer than a fortnight. Cost?"

"That'll be five a week, add the horse at twenty-five, a saddle with pad, the bit and reins, comes to fifty dollars, and that includes the one week of boarding."

"Thanks, and by the way, ever run into anyone around here by the name of Hiram Marlow?" Kindred asked.

"Yeah, he bought a Morgan team off me a few months back. Runs a small outfit out near the old Los Piños Indian Agency."

"Can you give me directions?"

"Not been out there myself but from what I understand, it's 'bout six or seven miles from here. There's an old trail that heads east out of town across from the hotel. Follow it 'til you come to Los Piños River and, I believe, Marlow and Carroll, the Indian he ranches with in a partnership, are about half a mile north just off the creek. What you wanting with Marlow?"

"Business," Kindred replied.

"What kind of business?"

"What business is it of yours?"

"Just wondering."

"Well, you can just go on wondering. In the meantime, spread the word I'm a tax collector."

As Kindred limped back to Tillman's boardinghouse, his anger rose, and his hands began to shake, as he thought about Carroll and Marlow together, an Indian and a white man in a partnership. *It's immoral if not illegal.* After changing his dressings, he rested on his bed for a minute and, then from under his pillow, he pulled the holstered pearl-handled pistol. He disassembled it, cleaned each part, and swiped an oiled cotton patch down the barrel. With the pistol fully reassembled, Kindred pulled back the hammer and successfully dry fired it. *Ready for action*, he thought. *And ready to go after not one but two individuals who gave false testimony. I'll send that Indian son-of-a-bitch Carroll to his happy hunting ground where he can meet up with the rest of those red niggers.*

Kindred loaded in six rounds, opened the door to his room, backed out into the hall to the stairway banister, and took aim at the triangle formed where the two walls in his room joined at the ceiling. *A thirty-yard shot*, he thought. *See if I can put the bullet into the triangle or between Marlow's eyes.* He held the pistol with his left hand shaking and tried to steady it with his other hand, the one missing the pinkie, ring, and middle fingers, grabbing his left wrist. The bullet hit two inches below its target, as the noise reverberated throughout the boardinghouse and a woman screamed from upstairs. *I need to squeeze lightly on the trigger*, Kindred thought, as he took aim for a second shot.

"Perfect," he said, looking at the hole in the plaster.

He backed away from the wall and fired off another shot.

"That one's for you, Carroll."

The proprietor rushed up the stairs. "What in hell is going on?"

"Just a little target practice," Kindred replied casually, as he set the gun on a small, nearby table.

"Sir, are you crazy? This isn't a shooting range or the site of a buffalo hunt. Do you know where you are?"

"Of course I do. In a courtroom. I just shot the private and the redskin. Both right between the eyes."

A half-dressed woman, her breasts bulging out from a pink corset, appeared out of breath at Kindred's door.

"I heard gun shots and . . . a bullet struck my wall upstairs. I was putting on my girdle, then *bang, bang*! I fell to the floor frightened to death."

"Ma'am, everything is under control," the proprietor said. "It's safe for you to return to your room."

Turning toward Kindred, he said, "Sir, you're scaring the hell out of other boarders. I'll have to take that pistol from you and lock it up at the front desk." The proprietor reached for the pistol on the table. Kindred jumped at him, missed the proprietor, but smashed into the table with his chest. The table fell into pieces to the floor as Kindred quickly grabbed the pistol.

"*You are not taking this pistol!*" Kindred screamed as he slipped it into its holster. The proprietor noticed the missing fingers.

"Sir, I'm going to have to call the sheriff."

"No, I won't fire the pistol again. Promise," Kindred said, trying to be polite.

The proprietor notice Kindred's hands shaking. "You OK, sir?"

"Just tuckered out. Thanks for asking. No more guns, I promise."

Petrified of more gunplay, the proprietor suggested Kindred "take a nap," and then added, "Just calm down, sir. I'll bring you a pot of tea. But no more damned gunplay."

Left alone, Kindred walked down the hall to the bathroom with the pistol in his pocket. He could tell from the yellow pus that one of his ulcers had become seriously infected. He changed the bandage and silently suffered the sting from the application of alcohol.

EIGHTEEN

MARLOW HOMESTEAD

Summer 1882

The next morning Kindred prepared to find Marlow. He rode the stallion out east from Gunnison toward Los Piños on what was, until recently, an Indian trail. The rutted road through the timber climbed gently toward a small pass and then dropped again into another shallow drainage. Someone had taken the time to riprap a low spot on the trail with oak branches where a small stream crossed it, and filled the potholes with rocks to assist passage in the spring. After stopping to water his horse, Kindred thought he heard a voice barking orders. He dismounted, tied his horse off the road in the thick timber, and walked toward the faint noise.

He came upon an open field, recently plowed. At the far end of the field, a man drove a Morgan team pulling a stone boat—a planked four-by-eight-foot platform bolted to two log runners, a contraption he recognized from his

Army days. Half filled with rocks, the boat moved forward twenty yards, stopped while the driver jumped off and rolled a boulder the size of a bowling ball onto the platform, and then moved forward again to load more rocks. When the driver had it loaded, he maneuvered the boat toward a gully on the east side of the field. The team backed the boat so that it tipped slightly backward over the lip of the gully. When the operator yelled and whipped the horses, the team surged forward, and the rocks slid backward off the boat into the gully.

For half an hour, Kindred watched the man in the field, waiting with a predator's patience, crawling slowly closer for confirmation that this was his quarry. The skilled driver collected, loaded, and dumped rocks before he slipped through the brush toward the gully. At this point Kindred confirmed his instincts, recognizing Marlow's short hair. Kindred knew he'd have to get himself closer to the dump site for a better shot. On the steep hillside he tried to move cautiously and quietly toward Marlow, but kept losing his footing. Only by grabbing a sagebrush root could he maintain his balance. He hesitated to move any closer for fear of spooking the horses and calling attention to his presence. He'd have to wait until Marlow's boat came closer to the edge of the field, where he'd have a clear shot at him. *Tomorrow*, Kindred thought.

Kindred spent a restless night as he considered the possible approaches to the killing of Marlow. *Should I use a carbine so as to allow a longer shot at Marlow? No, I can't steady its weight properly with my right hand. But with a pistol, not only can I better steady it, but I can fire off three shots in a matter of seconds rather than the single-shot carbine. I'll stay with the pistol but I'll have to get closer to*

Marlow. If Carroll shows up, I'll save three cartridges for the redskin.

The next morning he rode back to the homestead. He saw Marlow circling the stone boat in the middle of the field. He was working outward from the field's center, and with each circle he came closer to Kindred, who hid in the oak brush at the field's edge. *Two or three more circles*, Kindred thought, *and I'll be within firing range.*

Marlow emptied the boat at the gully's edge and returned to the middle of the field to repeat the process of collecting rocks. Kindred waited patiently for one more circle. The horses stopped within thirty-five yards of Kindred. Marlow wrapped the reins on the wooden post bolted to the front of the boat and stepped off to move a boulder toward the platform. Straining, Marlow rolled it onto the sled's edge and then leaned over to maneuver it to the center of the boat. He stood on the boat's deck to catch his breath.

Kindred's hands shook uncontrollably as he pulled back the hammer on his pearl-handled pistol, took careful aim, and squeezed off a round. And then another. The first bullet hit Marlow in the thigh. The second shot whistled as it ricocheted off a rock on the boat. The horses spooked and took off at a gallop in the opposite direction from the shots. Marlow fell back into the bed of the boat holding his leg as the team galloped across the field dragging behind the platform with Marlow laying on it. He fought to regain his footing and the reins of the runaway team. Blood from where a rock fragment struck him flowed down his arm. Kindred attempted a third shot, but the pistol misfired. Marlow knew enough to wait until the horses and boat had cleared the open field and entered the timber before rolling off onto the ground. The timber, he hoped, would stop the runaway team and provide some protection from the gunman. He looked out at the field and saw nothing.

Carroll, irrigating on the adjoining pasture, heard the shots and ran to secure the team, which had entangled themselves and the boat in the spruce grove. Meanwhile, from the other side of the field, Kindred saw that Marlow was out of shooting range and had taken cover in the trees.

Carroll found Marlow lying in the timber close to the field. "What Keller shooting at, you or team?" he asked, trying to catch his breath.

"Me, I think; got me in the thigh. They were pistol shots. I could tell by the pop."

"You shot in arm also. You OK?"

"The leg's OK and so is the arm, both flesh wounds, I think. Let's find that neighbor of ours. You got your pistol with you?"

"No, in cabin. I run and get both," Carroll said.

"Bring my carbine also. We might need more fire-power."

"Should we call Sheriff and let him capture Keller?" Carroll suggested.

"Hell, by the time we ride into town and find the sheriff, no doubt drunk in a bar, get him sober, and bring him out here, Keller will be long gone and back in Germany having a beer with his sausage."

Carroll ran for the cabin, while Marlow limped around the edge of the field, through the oak brush, sage, and trees to where he thought the shots had been fired. He came across fresh manure in some matted grass near a tree where a horse had been tied. He hollered to Carroll, who ran hunched over across the field with Marlow's carbine strapped to his back. Carroll looked at the manure and discovered nearby the hoofprints of a shod horse leading out to the road twenty yards away. In the road's dust, he carefully studied the prints.

"Whoever it is, he ride big horse. Look at size of shoe. Must be at least a seven." Carroll pointed to a new horse print. "And that right rear foot, it turn out. That not normal. It a injured horse. See if we find where Keller hide," he suggested.

They split to opposite sides of the field so as to cover more ground in the vicinity of the horse manure. Within ten minutes, Carroll found recently broken branches off a scrub oak bush, along with some matted grass. More importantly, in the late morning light he saw two brass shell casings and an unspent cartridge. He yelled to Marlow, who joined him and looked at the shell casings now in Carroll's hand.

"Forty-five-caliber shorts—for a Schofield. The unspent cartridge the same."

Marlow recognized the shell casings and cartridge, but nodded anyway. "Don't think it's our neighbor who's been doing the shooting today. The last time I saw Keller," he said, "he was packin' a Colt Peacemaker, same as ours, and riding a small, short-stepping and unshod mare."

"Who you think shoot at you?"

"Can't say I know for sure. But I have a suspicion," Marlow answered quietly as he continued to ponder the question.

Carroll broke the long silence. "Not difficult we find horse with the turned-out foot. He be a big horse, with big shoes. Maybe hardware store know who buy them. Also, with turned foot, maybe owner have it shod by blacksmith. We need go to town and do a hunt."

Carroll continued, "I see all three his horses. None had bad foot. Also he kill our calf with a Peacemaker. The shell casings we find today very different from Peacemaker shell."

"Maybe he owns a second weapon," Marlow volunteered.

"No. I guess he very poor and have little money for family to eat well. We go to town quick."

NINETEEN

The next morning the two men rode into Gunnison and made their first stop at the hardware store. They asked the manager if he stocked size six or seven horseshoes.

"With the toe grip or plain?" he asked.

"Plain," Carroll said.

"I got both."

"Within the last month or so, can you remember selling some plain number sixes or sevens to a customer?" Marlow asked.

"Hell, I must sell at least ten of them shoes in a month. What customer do you have in mind?"

"No one in particular," Marlow responded, "but if you had a horse that needed a corrective shoe because of an injury, where would you go in town?"

"Everyone I know uses Hank Perron, the owner of the livery stable. He's just down the street."

"Thanks," Marlow said, as the two men headed for the door.

Perron greeted the two men with a handshake that could squash a watermelon. "How's everything at the ranch, boys?"

"The rocks are doing well and growing like weeds. You need any? I'll trade you some high-grade boulders for a good saddle horse."

"Don't have no saddle horses right now, and I'm pretty well fixed for rocks."

"Hank, I understand you're about the only one in town who can fashion a corrective shoe for an injured horse, like a turned foot."

"Why? One of your Morgans got injured?"

"No, but I'm trying to find the owner of a large horse whose right hind foot turns out. Seen any horse like that?"

"Sure have, he's right back here in the stable," Perron responded.

They walked to the stall where Perron pointed to a muscular bay stallion. "One hell of a horse—almost sold him to your neighbor, that German fellow, looking for a stud. He thought my price too high. I wouldn't budge then, not for that big stallion. Last week I sold him to a former cavalry officer for half my asking price. I needed the money to pay off some debts. He asked the other day where you lived. Said he was a tax collector. Didn't look like no tax collector to me the way he was dressed in some frayed trousers. He rides most every day. Haven't seen him today, though."

"He live around here?" Marlow asked.

"No, said he was staying at Tillman's boardinghouse down the road."

"Name?"

"I asked him his name for the bill of sale but he never offered it. Just said to leave it blank and he'll fill it in later."

"Can you tell us anything else about this fellow?"

"He's of medium height, slight frame, and walks with a limp. The day he bought the horse, he had to use that women's mounting block over there," Perron said, pointing to a nearby foot-high wooden stump. "Even then he had a hard time pulling himself into the saddle with his right hand. He had a glove on it, and I kidded him that he didn't need it in this warm weather."

"What did he say?"

"Nothing, just stared at me. And another thing. He bought a saddle—a McClellan. I noticed that he put his gloved hand in the saddle's middle slot to help pull himself up. Maybe that's why he wanted to buy a damned McClellan. Most folks I do business with always ask for a normal saddle."

"He pack a weapon?" Carroll asked.

"A pistol."

"What kind?"

"Couldn't tell, but by the size of the holster, maybe a Peacemaker, but a fancy model. I could see it had a pearl handle."

Carroll and Marlow looked at each other and gave a slight nod. Then Marlow turned to Perron.

"I saw our neighbor Keller the other day. He's looking for a stud horse for his mares and desperate to find one. Told me he'd pay up to seventy-five dollars for a good one. I bet if the fellow you're talking about is looking to make a good profit, and he rode that stud horse out to Keller's place, the German would buy it on the spot. Pass the word on to that ex-cavalry officer. It'd help us also, having a stud horse nearby."

"I'll probably see him tomorrow, and I'll pass on the message. In the meantime, you boys take care. Turn those rocks of yours into hay and you'll see some good flesh on your livestock."

"We're workin' at it, Hank."

Carroll and Marlow walked to the Post Office before heading down to Tillman's boardinghouse to search for a former cavalry officer wearing a glove. A letter from Sarah awaited Marlow. Fearing the letter's contents, good news or bad, might divert his attention from the task at hand, Marlow placed the unopened letter in his breast pocket.

At the boardinghouse, Marlow told Tillman they were looking for a man who would have checked in about a week ago, walked with a slight limp, and wore a glove on his right hand.

"I can't be giving out the names of my boarders to everyone who asks," Tillman responded. Marlow pulled two one-dollar bills out of his pocket and placed them in front of Mr. Tillman, who smiled and said, "Mr. Fletcher is in room four, second floor. He's not in now. Asked about a doctor in town and then left about an hour ago."

"I need to leave him a note. Have any paper?" Marlow asked.

Marlow took the paper and wrote:

Dear Mr. Fletcher,

I seen dat horse you ride. I vanted to buy it two veeks ago, but da owner at da livery staple vant to much dollars. He tell me you da owner. Now I need stud horse like yours and vill pay big dollar for it. Can you be to my farm at Los Piños tomorrow morning and ve can talk? Get direction from Mr. Perron at da livery stable.

Tank you,
Franz Keller

"Put this in Mr. Fletcher's box for me. Thanks."

As the two men rode out of town back to their ranch, Carroll asked, "You think what I think?"

"It is Kindred for sure."

"What did you write in letter to Fletcher?"

"An invitation to ride out our way tomorrow and sell Keller his horse. I'm not going to hunt down Kindred here in town, and I want his visit to be in our territory and at a time that fits our schedule so we can do him some serious harm."

Carroll could only nod with a soft chuckle.

That evening they outlined their plan for the next day. After reviewing the details with each other, Marlow remembered Sarah's letter. He slit it open and read to himself.

Dear Hiram,

Thank you for your letter and the news of the homestead. How busy you must be building the cabin and clearing the fields. You must remember to look after your health.

We are busy at the store but father does not want to hire anyone to replace you. He is so hoping you will soon return! I haven't told him how happy you sound with your homestead. If I did tell him, he would probably hire someone to take on your past responsibilities, which would make it so much easier for the both of us.

Also Father has a nasty cough which he cannot rid himself of.

When I think of you every day, I want you back here in Ouray near me. But I also know that you are happy and successful where you are with Carroll and the prospect of your brother joining you.

Then I say to myself I want to be with you at the homestead so I can share your life, work beside you, and make you happy But I'm a city girl who knows nothing about homesteading and farming. I question if I can make you happy.

Stay in Ouray or live with you? When I balance out these two possibilities, I want to be with you at the homestead more than I want you here in Ouray. I am overjoyed at the thought of marriage, as you have suggested. Father, I believe, will approve, but my leaving Ouray would leave him with no help at the store. Certainly he can hire some good help and I could come visit him at least twice a year. I hope I am not too forward in my thoughts but I do want to be honest with you.

You cannot imagine how much I miss you. I go to the Post Office every day hoping for a letter from you. I know how busy you are, but you must write more often.

Good night, my dearest Hiram. I love you.
Sarah

TWENTY

Summer 1882

Hiram could not sleep thinking about Sarah's love and Kindred's impending capture. He was out of bed at first light, prepared breakfast for Carroll, and once again reviewed the plan to ambush Kindred.

The two partners left their horses at the cabin so that they or Kindred's horse wouldn't smell one another and nicker. In a thicket of oak brush just off the road that passed by Marlow's ranch on the way to Keller's place, they waited patiently for Kindred to approach. Both men carried pistols, fully loaded.

They waited almost two hours and had about decided Kindred had not taken the bait. As they emerged from the brush hideout, Carroll raised his hand. He whispered to Marlow, "I hear horse." The men went back into the brush.

Within two minutes they could see Kindred riding his stallion on the road. He wore a tan blouse tucked into a pair of faded and frayed cavalry trousers. Some gray hair had escaped from under his black floppy hat. A dirty white pillow covered his saddle and a holster hung from his left side. He rode slowly, looking carefully to both sides of the road.

Marlow and Carroll sprang from the oak brush with pistols drawn. Standing in front of Kindred's horse, Marlow ordered, "Hold your horse up and put your hands over your head." Kindred reined his horse to a stop, and before he could reach for his pistol, Carroll shouted from his rear, "Put hands *higher*! Remove glove with left hand and throw hat on ground. You move toward holster and this forty-five slug find a new home in your chest. Now slide off horse on left side."

Kindred threw his right leg over the back of his horse, leaned his chest on the saddle for balance, removed his left foot from the stirrup, and slid off the horse. A dark stain discolored the crotch of his trousers. The dirty pillow fell to the ground beside him.

"Now walk slowly toward me. *Keep those hands up*," Marlow shouted.

Marlow looked past Kindred to Carroll, who had remained behind Kindred. "Ben, if it weren't for the scruffy beard and untrimmed mustache and hair, I'd swear we were looking at the No Finger Chief. He always carried a pearl-handled Schofield pistol. Check his holster and see what this fellow is packing."

As Kindred faced Marlow's cocked pistol, Carroll came up from behind, unsnapped the cover on Kindred's holster, and removed the pistol. He patted him down in a search for other weapons.

"A beautiful nickel-plated Schofield with a pearl handle and some initials—J. P. K.," Carroll said before placing the pistol under his waist belt. Then he pulled from his saddlebag an old rawhide lace and wrapped Kindred's wrists behind his back.

"Well, if it isn't Colonel Kindred. You're a long way from home. What brings you to our neighborhood?" Marlow asked.

"Was on my way to see your neighbor about my horse."

"You recognize me, Colonel?"

"You're Private Marlow, the one who testified against me at my court-martial."

Turning to Carroll, Marlow asked, "And this man here?"

"My Indian interpreter from the Uncompahgre."

"Colonel, you've got a hell of a memory for a washed-up old Army officer. By chance, were you out here the other day using me for target practice?"

"Not me. Had to be someone else."

"Let's all of us take a walk over to the pasture beyond the trees," Marlow said.

Carroll led the stallion into the trees where he tied him. Marlow and Kindred followed.

"Are you planning to kill me?" Kindred asked as if pleading for his life.

"The thought never entered my mind, but now that you mention it, I'll give it serious consideration," Marlow said with a smirk.

"Me too," Carroll added.

"I want to know why you tried to kill me two days ago," Marlow asked.

"You're the one whose false testimony ruined my career."

"What was false?"

"You testified in my court-martial that Running Bear presented no threat to me when I shot him in self-defense. You lied when you said Running Bear was on his knees. You knew damned well he was standing and was a threat to my life in the same way he tried to strangle me inside my tent. And besides, I was following orders—orders from General Sheridan."

"Sure you were—you had to kill Running Bear to protect him and his band. What you really did was lie and fail to take responsibility for your own actions. In fighting Indians throughout your career you've always raised the level of violence and cruelty among the Indians *and* our troops. You call Indians savages. What are you? Some sort of Christian savior?"

"And who are you, an ex-private, to judge me or my actions?"

"When someone is out to kill me, I'll act as judge and jury."

"And your verdict?

"Guilty as hell."

"Guilty for killing a redskin in self-defense?"

"There you go again imagining things," Marlow said as he and Carroll faced Kindred. "Now, Colonel, we're going to re-create that scene outside your headquarters in Utah Territory where, as you testified, Running Bear presented a threat to your life. Suppose for a minute you're Running Bear, on your knees and with your hands tied behind your back, and I'm you in this situation standing to your front. And when you get on your knees, I'm going to shout '*leap*.' I want you to leap at me as if you wanted to kill me. Now, Mr. Carroll, help the colonel get to his knees."

Carroll slammed into Kindred's chest with his shoulder, forcing Kindred hard to the ground. As he hit,

Kindred could feel the pressure of the rawhide lace release from his wrists. Acting as if his hands were bound tight, Kindred struggled to get to his knees. Carroll leaned forward, grabbed Kindred's collar, and pulled him to his knees. Instantly, Kindred sprang at Carroll's legs and tackled him to the ground. He pulled the Schofield pistol from Carroll's waist, leaned back, and shouted, "*I'll kill you, you red bastard!*"

It took Marlow only a second to pull back the hammer on his pistol and fire one shot point-blank into Kindred's forehead, just above the left eyebrow. The back of his head disappeared. A burst of brain tissue, blood, and bone exited from what remained of Kindred's skull. He fell onto his back, his mouth open, his pearl-gray eyes staring at the sky as they sunk into his head.

Marlow turned to Carroll. "The crazy son of a bitch thought you were Running Bear. I know you wanted the honors, but he was about to kill you."

"Not possible. Look, chamber and cylinder both empty."

"You knew that?"

"Of course. You think Indian walk around with loaded pistol under his belt?"

Both men laughed as they put a bear hug on each other. Then Marlow offered, "You want his scalp?"

"Not much remain. What I do with small patch of gray hair?"

"Let's fetch the stone boat, and we'll take Kindred to that small grassy clearing up near where the ditch comes onto the ranch. It's a nice spot for a cemetery, though I doubt if Kindred will appreciate the scenery."

The two men placed Kindred on the boat's platform, and, after making some minor repairs to it, headed to the top of the ranch. They dug the grave, wrapped Kindred in a canvas tarp, and placed him facing east before shoveling the grave closed. On an aspen tree behind the grave, Marlow carved into the bark the initials "J. P. K." and the date "8-27-82."

At supper, the two men said very little at first. Carroll volunteered, "You're lucky with your leg wound. Bullet went in and out through muscle without hitting bone."

"For sure. If that bastard had more fingers on his shooting hand I might be the one up in the cemetery with different initials on the tree."

"Maybe not good we kill Kindred. Maybe we take him under guard to sheriff in town."

Marlow shot an angry look at Carroll. "Kindred tried to kill me two days ago and you today. Remember? Involve the sheriff, and that would have meant more court testimony, more questions, more lawyers, and less justice. He had his trial today, and we carried out the sentence.

"On a more pleasant subject," Marlow continued, "I'm going to return to Ouray tomorrow and see my lady friend. I think she will marry me. If she says yes, I'll return here with a new bride. You got any problems having a woman around the place? I know she's handy, also a better cook than me."

Carroll laughed and responded, "I hope she say yes. Also after your brother arrives, he help you to cook." Then Carroll turned serious and asked Marlow, "You think folks in town want to know where is Kindred?"

"Maybe Tillman and Perron will be looking for Fletcher if he's left some bills behind. I'll go tell Perron I bought that stud horse from the former cavalry officer. Also I'll tell him I saw that so-called tax collector boarding a stage to Salida, and before he left he asked that I 'settle up with you.' I can use the money that we took from Kindred's pocket. I'll repeat the same message and offer to Tillman. I can't think of anyone else looking for him except maybe the gatekeeper in hell," Marlow said before suggesting they get a good night's sleep.

That night, Marlow's dream of sleeping with Sarah replaced the recurring nightmare of the Comanche attack in Texas. Now with the colonel dead, a new horse to ride, and the plan to marry Sarah, Marlow could put his mind toward the prospect of a successful cattle business and a family. The blue of Sarah's eyes filled his dreams.

ACKNOWLEDGMENTS

The idea for this novel came from my research on the Ute tribe, specifically the northern bands from the White River Valley and the Uncompahgre Valley, for my book *The Utes Must Go*. I tried to imagine their grief as they were forced at gunpoint to leave their traditional homeland in Colorado, one guaranteed to them by two US presidents. One of the major characters in my book, Colonel Joseph Kindred, is modeled in part after the early life of Ranald S. Mackenzie, the famous Indian fighter who the Army charged with moving the Ute to Utah. I am indebted to Charles M. Robinson III for his book *Bad Hand: A Biography of General Ranald S. Mackenzie*.

Throughout the process of researching for this book, I have received guidance and assistance from the staffs at the Denver Public Library (Western History Room), the Center of Southwest Studies (Fort Lewis College), and the US Military Academy (West Point).

Drafts of this novel were read and improved by a talented number of writers and editors: Kent Nelson, Betsy Armstrong, Kathy Kaiser, and the gang at Girl Friday Productions (Susan Wilson Hulett, Christina Henry de

Tessan, Tegan Tigani, Michelle Hope Anderson, and Leah Tracosas Jenness).

Along the way, I had the encouragement of my good friends Bill Adler, Syd Nathan, and Steve and Margaret Horn. And as always, my loyal secretary of many years, Anne Price, improved the story line with her ideas and suggestions. I'd also like to thank Fred Chiaventone for his expertise on nineteenth-century Army weapons and Lisa Atchison for creating the website.

Finally, running a cattle ranch while trying to write a novel are two endeavors that do not fit well together. Thanks to my wife, Deedee, for stepping in at all times to help with ranch responsibilities (fixing fences, irrigating, building repairs, doctoring animals, etc.) while I struggled over the complexities of a compound sentence.

ABOUT THE AUTHOR

Peter Decker received a PhD in American history from Columbia University, and taught at both Columbia and Duke University. After relocating to Colorado, he served as Commissioner of Higher Education, Commissioner of Agriculture, and a director of the Federal Reserve Bank of Denver. In addition to nonfiction publications about the history of the West, including the award-winning book *Old Fences, New Neighbors*, Decker self-published *Saving the West*, a satirical novel. Decker makes his home on a ranch in Colorado.